Shannon switched on her brightest, most professional smile. ‘You’ve got it all wrong, Mr Jacobsen—of course I don’t dislike you.’

‘I wonder why I’m finding it difficult to believe a single word uttered by those gorgeous lips?’ Dane murmured. ‘And what would it feel like to have the truth from them?’ In a single swift movement he planted both hands about her waist, pulling her hard against his body.

‘Mr Jacobsen, for goodness’ sake! What on earth do you think you’re doing?’

Something that’s got very little to do with goodness,’ he grunted. ‘Something I’ve been wanting to do for quite some time. You present a highly intriguing challenge, Miss Shannon Lea—and I intend to find out what lurks behind that icy-cool exterior.’

Another book you will enjoy
by RACHEL ELLIOT

FANTASY OF LOVE

Local vet Jamie Oliver dismissed Casey on sight as a hopelessly sophisticated career girl just playing at country living, at the possible expense of her new pony. But, for someone who detested her kind, he seemed to be sparing a lot of time for her. . .

WINTER CHALLENGE

BY

RACHEL ELLIOT

MILLS & BOON LIMITED
ETON HOUSE 18–24 PARADISE ROAD
RICHMOND SURREY TW9 1SR

First published in Great Britain 1991
by Mills & Boon Limited

This edition 1992

ISBN 0 263 77436 8

Set in 10½ on 12 pt Linotron Plantin
01-9202-53272
Typeset in Great Britain by Centracet, Cambridge
Made and printed in Great Britain

CHAPTER ONE

TALL and proud he stood, his hawklike features stern as he surveyed the kingdom that was his. Unmoving, he seemed part of the very landscape he stood in, his eyes deep and clear as the blue sea before him, his shoulder-length hair just as golden as the sun burning far above in an azure sky. He was powerfully built, the muscles rippled beneath the tanned skin of his arms as he raised his hands skywards in a gesture of fierce possession. One of the silent watchers, a slender young woman with hair the colour of a fiery sunset, bowed her head in unconscious submissiveness. This was the Viking, and he had laid claim to all that was truly his. All was as it should be.

'Cut! That's a wrap.'

Shannon's sherry-coloured eyes danced with a mixture of amusement and pleasure as the short, rather portly director gave the classic command. His smile might be a little self-conscious, but she was close enough to see the glint of real satisfaction in his pale blue eyes. He was entitled to his moment of pride; shooting had gone well on the set of *The Viking*—astonishingly well considering it had been done on a ludicrously small budget and with television crews much more accustomed to slapstick children's shows than gritty drama.

'Michael's been reading his book of *Things a Director's Supposed to Say* again,' a voice murmured somewhere above her ear, and Shannon turned with a grin to the tall blonde woman at her side.

'Don't be heartless, Merry,' she scolded teasingly. 'This is his moment of glory.'

Merry nodded, sending artlessly styled golden curls bobbing about her heart-shaped face.

'I know. I just wish he hadn't felt a pressing need to turn himself into some sort of Hollywood-director clone for this production. After all, he's been working here for centuries, and I bet no one's ever heard him say "Cut, that's a wrap", before.'

Shannon glanced back towards the set, her eyes narrowing as she watched actors and crew clustering round one tall, powerful-looking figure like bees round a honeypot.

'Perhaps he's never had to work with anyone like Dane Jacobsen before,' she said flatly. 'He's enough to make anyone feel a little insecure.'

Merry chuckled. 'So you still haven't decided to give the poor guy a break, even for the last day on set?'

Shannon turned incredulous eyes on the other woman.

'"Poor guy"?' she echoed in amazement. 'Dane Jacobsen a "poor guy"? Give me a break, Merry, the man's an ego on legs.'

Merry pursed her lips in a silent whistle. 'But what legs!' she murmured with heartfelt appreciation. 'And the rest of him's pretty wickedly structured too, if you ask me.'

Shannon gave an unladylike snort. 'He'd certainly never have to ask you, that's for sure. He's only too aware of his own charms.'

'So you do admit the man's gorgeous?' Merry slid

her a considering look. 'That's a major concession on your part, surely?'

Shannon shook her head. 'Not at all.' Her eyes were drawn back to the set, where Dane was still holding court. Somehow he was able to dwarf everyone else around him, not just by his size, though that was considerable, but by sheer presence, so that, even though he was surrounded by half a dozen or more people, the casual onlooker would be aware only of him.

It was always the same wherever he went—people were drawn inexorably to him, as though some of his charisma could rub off on them if they could just get close enough. Shannon had, rather uncharitably, put it down to the lure of the man's fame—people simply liked to be close to the famous. But now, as she watched, she was forced to acknowledge there was more to it than that. Standing in the centre of the set, Dane Jacobsen was a still, enigmatic presence, aloof and apart from the restless, chattering throng surrounding him.

As though running a mental checklist, Shannon took in the burnished golden hair rippling in thick waves to his staggeringly broad shoulders, then let her eyes wander down over his powerful chest to narrow hips and long, muscular legs. He was built like a Greek god—or like one of the Norse warlords of old, and it wasn't hard to believe the publicity material which said he was descended from the Vikings. Unthinkingly she let her eyes stray to his face, only to flinch abruptly as she realised his deep blue eyes were focused on her, their expression strangely sardonic. Dammit, he'd seen her looking at him—that really rankled. She looked away, but not before her normally pale skin had flooded with colour, and it was all the more infuriating to know he'd seen that too.

'You were saying?' Merry said drily, having witnessed the interesting little exchange.

'I was saying,' Shannon strove to sound as dignified as it was possible to sound for someone who was blushing like a schoolgirl, 'that of course I admit the man's gorgeous. That's never been in any doubt—particularly to him. It's his arrogance I can't abide.'

'I don't know,' Merry mused aloud. 'I quite like a touch of arrogance in men.'

'A touch is one thing,' Shannon returned wryly, 'But with him it's one hundred per cent.'

'In which case I don't suppose you desperately want to join the crowd of people currently queueing up to tell him how wonderful he was?' Merry gave a little chuckle as Shannon rolled her eyes heavenwards. 'No? Then let's go back to the make-up room. I'd like to get cleared up so I can join the others at the end-of-shoot bash this evening.'

As they walked out of the studio, Merry glanced at her thoughtfully. 'Are you sure you won't change your mind about coming tonight? You've worked just as hard as everyone else on this production, even though. . .'

'Even though I *am* just a freelance?' Shannon smiled ruefully as she completed the sentence. It wasn't the first time she'd heard that kind of comment.

'You know I didn't mean that the way you've made it sound,' Merry protested, and Shannon made a quick, dimissive gesture.

'It's OK—I know we're still a breed apart as far as many people are concerned. But no one here has treated me as though I were anything but a permanent staff member, so don't have any worries on that score.'

'Then will you come tonight?'

Shannon shook her head. 'No—but only because I've got a long drive ahead of me. I'd like to get on the road as soon as possible.'

Merry frowned. 'And I've asked you to cover for the last half-hour—that was selfish of me.'

'Don't be silly. Another thirty minutes won't make any difference—anyway, I'll need that to get organised. My stuff's still scattered everywhere.'

Merry eyed her doubtfully. 'Well, if you're absolutely sure. . .'

'I am, I am! Now go on, go home and make yourself even more beautiful than you already are—knock their eyes out at the party.'

Exactly thirty minutes later, Shannon packed the last two brushes into an already crammed hold-all and glanced quickly round the small room, checking for anything she might have missed first time round. So far, so good. She'd already phoned home to check her answering-machine for messages, now she was free to head north. With clear roads and a good wind behind her, she should reach the cottage in around four or five hours, and frankly she couldn't wait. It was only a long-weekend break, perhaps, but after the never-ending block of work she'd taken on since turning freelance she was more than ready for the rest.

She gave a little sigh. Working freelance was enormously enjoyable for the most part—gave her the chance to travel, to meet new people and see new places, but there was an inevitable insecurity, too. So far she'd found plenty of work, but the television world was a notoriously fickle one, with an extremely efficient grapevine. Without the safety net of a staff job, she had to be even more than usually careful when dealing with the fragile egos of those who appeared before the cameras—one adverse comment and she could find herself facing nothing but closed doors. It had happened to other freelancers, she knew.

She was shaken from her reverie by a sharp, peremptory rap on the door.

'Anyone around?'

She closed her eyes against a brief flare of irritation. She really had thought she'd heard the last of that voice. It was no comfort at all to know she was probably the only female in existence who didn't thrill to its rich, deep tones, who was left completely unmoved by its huskily sensual undertones.

Dane Jacobsen was one of the best known and most accomplished actors of his generation, so it had been a real coup for the tiny television station to secure his services for a drama serial on the Vikings, to be shot in Cumbria. Shannon had met him for the first time when he'd arrived to film the pilot episode, and her dislike for the golden Adonis had been instant. He was just too beautiful, too confident, too sure of himself. She couldn't imagine he could ever have had a single moment of nervous insecurity in his whole charmed life.

'I'm here, Mr Jacobsen. Did you want something?' Pulling on a warm suede jacket, she summoned up a lukewarm smile as he strode into the room, instantly dominating the place with his presence.

'A haircut,' he said tersely, and the abruptness of his tone set her teeth on edge. Who did he think he was, throwing commands about like that as though he owned the place?

She shook her head. 'I'm just about to leave.'

'So I see.' His eyes flickered over the bulging hold-all. 'Then you'd better get on with the job quickly.'

She bridled at his tone, irritated hugely by his assumption that she'd simply drop everything to dance to his bidding.

'Mr Jacobsen,' she said carefully, 'as I believe I intimated just a moment ago, I'm just about to leave.'

'And as I intimated just a moment ago,' his voice was coldly mocking as he threw her words back at her, 'I need a haircut.' The deep sea-blue eyes were unreadable, yet in a strange way she felt pinned to the spot by them, like a butterfly trapped and doomed to die.

Shannon took a deep breath, mentally counting to ten. Despite her fiery auburn curls, she very rarely lost her temper—largely because she'd learnt over the years to put a tight lid on seething emotions in public, keeping explosions solely for when she was by herself. Now she could feel the tell-tale simmering of indignation deep inside, and knew that with very little provocation this bad mood could develop into a Class A volcano.

'Look, Mr Jacobsen,' she said evenly, 'I really don't wish to be rude, but I do want to get away.'

'And the longer you stand here arguing, the longer it will take you to get away.'

She looked very pointedly at her watch. 'I'm no longer on duty.'

'And may not be ever again as far as this company's concerned.'

His words made her gasp as though he'd flung a bucket of cold water over her.

'I beg your pardon?'

'I think you heard what I said.' The blue eyes studied her implacably.

'Are you threatening me?' Even now she could barely believe the evidence of her own ears.

He smiled lazily, but it was a cool, unfeeling smile. His strong, even teeth glinted white against the bronze of his skin, and with a peculiar detachment Shannon found herself wondering if the tan had come from a sun-bed or even a bottle. It was unlikely. The colour looked too glowingly real. He'd probably achieved it on a pleasant little trip to the Bahamas.

'Shall we say I'm reminding you of your place in the scheme of things,' he said, narrowing his eyes. 'Your. . .very temporary place.'

Shannon shook her head wonderingly. 'You'd complain to the management if I refused to cut your hair?' she guessed. 'But that's despicable.'

He shrugged, unmoved by her opinion. 'You have a choice.'

And oh, how she'd love to use that choice and tell him to take a hike, she thought longingly. But he had her between a rock and a hard place, and the look in his eyes told her only too clearly that he knew it.

'All right,' she muttered at last, with very poor grace. 'Sit down there with your back to the sink.' She turned away to throw her jacket on to a chair, then walked through to the adjoining storeroom to collect shampoo and a towel. When she returned, the sight that met her eyes made her gasp involuntarily.

'Is there a problem?' he asked calmly, continuing

to unbutton his faded denim shirt before her horrified gaze.

'You don't need to—to——' She gestured vaguely with one hand, dismayed to feel a rush of warmth invade her cheeks. What on earth was wrong with her all of a sudden? She was a make-up artist, for goodness' sake—she'd seen any number of half-naked male actors in her time, but she'd never reacted like this before.

'I prefer it this way.' He shrugged the shirt off his ludicrously broad shoulders. He tossed the garment casually on to a chair, and her eyes were drawn inexorably to his broad expanse of chest. She was surprised to see it was covered by a thick mat of soft fair hair—somehow she'd have expected someone as blond as him to have smooth, hairless skin. The covering of hair did nothing to disguise the rippling muscles, as he moved to the chair she'd indicated, and she swallowed painfully. She might be growing to detest the man more with every passing second, but she doubted there was a woman alive who could deny his sheer male beauty, or fail to be drawn to it on the most basic level.

'Don't bother washing it.'

Dane was either unaware of her stunned reaction, or else was simply taking it for granted, she thought irritably. He was obviously well accustomed to women going to pieces in his presence.

'Just chop a bit off.'

Shannon shook her head. If she was going to do the job at all, professional pride demanded she do it properly and, for hair as thick and luxuriant as his, 'just chopping a bit off' wouldn't do at all.

'Sit down,' she said curtly.

He slid her a coolly measuring look, clearly not accustomed to being told what to do by a mere make-up artist, but to her relief he did as he was bid, lowering himself into the chair and sliding down to tilt his head back into the sink.

'This is the first time you've attended to me since I've been here,' he commented, his expression speculative as he glanced up at her. 'Why?'

'Sheer coincidence.' She tucked a towel round his neck, not quite managing to meet his knowing look. It was true she'd avoided him, had gladly left him to Merry, but it hadn't occurred to her that he might be aware of that. She wasn't even sure why she'd been so reluctant to come into contact with him. Some deep-down instinct she'd never properly investigated had simply made her back off. Now she began to wonder about that; it couldn't simply be because she'd disliked him, since she'd disliked clients before, but that hadn't prevented her from giving them the same professional treatment she gave to everyone. No, if it came right down to it, she simply hadn't wanted to touch him. The realisation made her lips curve in a self-mocking little grin.

'Would you care to share the joke?'

She shook her head, afraid that if she attempted to speak she'd start to laugh. How could she tell him that, while women all over the country would do just about anything even to be in the same room as him, she, Shannon Lea, didn't want to touch him? He would undoubtedly consider her certifiable.

Reaching behind him, she turned on the taps, mixing the water-flow to a reasonable temperature, then slid her hands deep into his lion's mane, pushing the molten gold back from his forehead. It was a movement she'd made a million times before, yet as soon as her fingers came into contact with his thick, silky hair she felt a jolt as though an electric current had shot right through her, making her start back in surprise.

'Something wrong?' He twisted his head slightly to look up at her

'No.' She blinked twice, wondering what on earth had caused the incredible sensation. Static electricity, perhaps? No, that caused only a tiny prickling sensation, and she'd experienced that before, in any case. This had been much more powerful—enough to make her knees go weak. She glanced surreptitiously downward, wondering if he'd felt it too, but his expression gave nothing away. With a tiny shrug she started working shampoo into his hair, but fear of the same thing happening again made her fingers a little more tentative than usual.

'Can't you press any harder?' His voice was coldly impatient. 'I like to have my scalp massaged properly, not tickled.'

Gritting her teeth, she dug her fingers right in, only just resisting the temptation to rake her nails across his head. 'Better?' she enquired with saccharine sweetness. He gave a little grunt of pleasure.

'Much. You have a very sure touch, Miss Lea.'

Normally she'd have shampooed his hair twice, but his compliment had rattled her badly, or perhaps it was the deep and husky voice he'd said it in, and she quickly rinsed the lather off, pulling the towel up over his head to blot excess water.

'Where are you going this weekend?'

'Why?' She shot him a suspicious glance as she began combing his hair.

'Have I stumbled on some dark and desperate secret?' His eyes narrowed speculatively as they watched her in the mirror. 'Are you heading off for a dirty weekend with the managing director?'

'Certainly not!' She was scandalised by the very idea, especially since the MD was a delightfully avuncular man, certainly old enough to be her father. 'It's no secret. I'm going skiing with a friend.'

'Male or female?'

The comb skidded over his slippery hair.

'I really don't see that it's any of your business, Mr Jacobsen.'

'So you're ashamed of your companion?'

Her hand stilled as she looked down at him in outraged astonishment. 'Ashamed?' she repeated incredulously. 'That's a ridiculous thing to suggest!'

'Is it?' The sea-blue eyes gazing back at her were coolly assessing, and it took considerable effort on her part not to look away. 'Then why are you so reluctant to admit who you're meeting?'

'I don't see that I have to "admit" anything,' she shot back hotly, stung by his words and struggling once again to contain her temper. She couldn't remember ever having met anyone with quite this capacity for rousing her to anger, she thought abstractedly. 'My actions and my choice of companions are entirely my own affair, and frankly I don't see any reason to divulge any information about either.'

As soon as the words were out Shannon heartily wished them unspoken. She was being stupidly short-sighted in snapping at this man. He was the most infuriating person she'd ever had the misfortune to encounter, but probably also the most influential. In truth she couldn't afford to antagonise him, and that angered her still more.

She took a deep breath, mentally counting to ten, then adding another twenty for safety's sake.

'Look,' she said steadily, 'I'm going skiing with my best friend. She's a twenty-seven year-old female, just the same age as me, her name is Kelly Adam, she's a television camerawoman, and we've been friends for years. OK?'

'That's better.' He nodded with a peculiarly male satisfaction at her capitulation, and she felt her stomach muscles clench in irritation. 'What about men?'

'I beg your pardon?' She stared down at him uncomprehendingly.

'Men,' he repeated, sardonic amusement glinting in his eyes. 'The opposite sex. Since you're apparently not packing your own on this trip, I take it you and Kelly will be on the look-out for handsome ski-bums?'

Shannon was all but overwhelmed by the urge to slap his face—just who in sweet heaven did he think he was? Only her resolve not to irritate him prevented her from letting the scissors stray towards his temptingly close ears, and she swallowed hard on the furious retort which jumped to her lips.

'I hate to disillusion you, Mr Jacobsen——' to her relief her light, careless laugh sounded almost genuine '—but women do occasionally manage to be in the company of other women without any thought of men. It so happens Kelly and I have been looking forward to this weekend, and I guarantee that men will play no part in it at all.'

'You seem very sure of that.'

'I am. For one thing, Kelly's very happily involved

in a relationship and has been for some time, so I'm quite convinced her eyes won't stray towards any ski-bums, no matter how handsome.'

'And what about you? Are you so inviolable that no man might dare to venture near?' The blue eyes studied her lazily in the mirror, and she had the strangest sensation he was toying with her as a cat would a mouse before a kill. But how would he react if she were to tell him the truth? she wondered distantly. What would he say if she told him of the background that had left her with a deep and enduring mistrust of men?

'Not inviolable, Mr Jacobsen,' she said at last, with a falsely bright smile. 'Simply not interested.'

'Or is it that you're immune?' he said slowly. 'Are you a man-hater, Shannon Lea?'

She flinched as though cut physically by his words. 'That's a terrible thing to suggest.'

'Is it?' He twisted slightly in the chair to look up at her. 'Isn't that why you've avoided me like the very plague ever since I've been here?'

She closed her eyes briefly, rocked by a reaction that was incredulity and outrage in equal parts. Oh, the sheer male arrogance of him—the unbelievable conceit!

'Mr Jacobsen,' she forced herself to speak slowly and calmly, refusing to let him know he'd just lit a tinder within her, 'it may have escaped your notice that you were not the only member of the cast—come to that, you weren't the only male, either. Despite what you apparently think, I certainly didn't avoid you intentionally and, in any case, if your theory were correct, then surely I'd have avoided all the male actors?'

He shrugged, ignoring the slight hint of triumph in her reasoning. 'There was nothing to avoid,' he said matter-of-factly. 'None of them would have provided any kind of challenge to your tightly guarded female bastion.'

She gasped aloud, completely and utterly taken aback by his easy dismissal of every other man in the cast. 'Whereas you would, I suppose?'

The undisguised sarcasm in her voice sparked no answering reaction in him other than an almost imperceptible raising of one eyebrow, before he said, 'Obviously you thought so.'

She shook her head, finding it hard to believe the conversation. 'Mr Jacobsen, I hardly think my alleged avoidance of you is justification enough for labelling me a man-hater.'

'"Alleged avoidance?" Lady, I've seen you scuttle from the room as if your butt were on fire simply because I've walked in.' The deep blue eyes held an unmistakable challenge. 'I'm not accustomed to being treated that way—and I'm not crazy about it.'

In a strange way Shannon found she was almost impressed by the strength of his ego—an ego that was apparently impervious to self-doubt or criticism. It must be truly wonderful to walk through life guarded by such a shield. She'd encountered any number of stars who thought themselves special simply because of their fame, but this one was clearly the king of them all. He simply couldn't believe anyone could be less than bowled over by him. Little wonder, really, she acknowledged ruefully—she'd seen women in the building all but swoon at his feet every time he walked down the corridor. They all treated him as a golden idol, and he'd obviously begun to believe it himself.

Well, Shannon had never met an idol yet who didn't possess feet of clay, and there was nothing to suggest he was the exception.

Once again she took a deep breath to steady the anger churning within, and summoned up her steadiest voice.

'I really don't know where you got the idea that I've been avoiding you,' she said with laudable calm. 'The truth is, I've simply been trying not to step on Merry's toes. After all, she is chief make-up artist here. I merely assist.'

'And Merry always sees to the leading actors?'

Unthinkingly she shook her head, then belatedly realised her mistake and coloured. 'Not always, but. . .'

'But in this case you decided it would be a good idea to leave me entirely in her more than capable hands?'

She nodded.

'I wonder why?' he mused aloud. 'You don't strike me as the type who'd be unduly overwhelmed by my so-called fame. So what makes you dislike me?'

She busied herself with the scissors, studying his hair intently. In her job she was accustomed to boosting fragile egos and bolstering shaky morales, but it went against the grain to tell outright lies. In this case, however, she didn't really have much choice, and the realisation rankled.

'I don't dislike you, Mr Jacobsen,' she returned at last, with all the conviction she could muster. 'It's merely been the luck of the draw that Merry's seen to you every time.'

'The draw from a loaded deck of cards,' he muttered darkly, and she glanced down at him in some surprise. Why should he care that she'd avoided him? Why on earth should it matter to him? He could expect fawning adoration wherever he went—surely he couldn't be so in need of blanket adulation that one heretic in the court could upset him?

She shook her head, silently giving up the battle to understand. She wasn't an actor, and she'd never be able to fully comprehend what made the breed tick, even though she worked with their number practically every day. Right about now a tactful change of subject seemed in order.

'So,' she said brightly, 'where are you off to now that we've finished shooting *The Viking*?'

His eyes narrowed, and for a second she thought he'd refuse to follow her lead, but to her relief he shrugged.

'That depends on whether or not we get the green light for a full series, and that won't be known for a couple of months. Otherwise my diary's clear. I thought I'd take a break.'

'Resting?' She glanced down at him shrewdly. 'I thought actors hated inactivity.'

'I didn't say I'd be inactive,' he returned, irritation darkening his features. 'And it won't be resting—not in the way most actors use the term, anyway.'

'So what will you do?' The cutting complete, she began blow-drying his hair.

'Perhaps I'll come skiing with you.' He ducked abruptly. 'Careful with that thing—you're burning my ear.'

'Sorry.' She moved the drier and continued working on his hair, one part of her mind marvelling at how perfectly the golden locks fell back into place. The other part was reeling at the very idea of Dane

Jacobsen on the snowy slopes of Glenshee with her. Not that he'd be out of place—on the contrary, he would look entirely at home among the mountains—but the very notion of spending time with him was enough to horrify her. She met his eyes in the mirror and summoned up a weak, unconvincing smile. His answering look told her he knew exactly what she'd been thinking.

'You really do dislike me,' he said thoughtfully. 'I wonder why.'

She swept the towel from the back of his neck, flicking away a few strands of hair. She'd done well—the shorter style suited him, throwing his hawklike features into stark, uncompromising relief. Ironically she felt a tiny pang of regret for the long Viking locks, though she couldn't have said why. But then, as she was fast coming to realise, that was par for the course really, since nothing appeared to make much sense where Dane Jacobsen was concerned.

She switched on her brightest, most professional smile. 'You've got it all wrong, Mr Jacobsen—of course I don't dislike you. If I've been a little abrupt, then I sincerely apologise. It's just that I'm in a hurry to get away.'

'I wonder why I'm finding it difficult to believe a single word uttered by those gorgeous lips,' he murmured. 'And what would it feel like to have the truth from them?' In a single, swift movement he rose to his feet, and she gave a squawk of outraged protest as he planted both hands about her waist, pulling her hard against his body.

'Mr Jacobsen, for goodness' sake! What on earth do you think you're doing?'

'Something that's got very little to do with goodness,' he grunted. 'Something I've been wanting to do for quite some time. You present a highly intriguing challenge, Miss Shannon Lea—and I intend to find out what lurks beneath that icy-cool exterior.'

Even as she struggled he was lifting her clear off her feet as easily as though she were made of thistledown. Enraged by his presumption, she longed to land him a good smack on the face, famous actor or no famous actor, but he had her arms pinned to her sides, and his strength was far greater than hers.

'If you don't let me down this instant, Mr Jacobsen, I'll. . .'

'You'll what?' His eyebrows quirked humorously, 'You'll scream? Then I'd better do something to prevent you.' His mouth took hers and she clenched her hands into tight fists, desperately fighting the urge within herself to clutch at his waist. She was all too horribly aware of the traitorous reactions of her own body as her breasts, covered only by the thin material of a sweatshirt, pressed against his naked chest.

The scent of shampoo, clean and tangy, still clung to him, but there was another more masculine note to the aroma, a note that made her heady with its faint hint of warm male skin. His kiss was like no other she'd ever experienced—not a caress, but a declaration of possession, as though he was staking a claim to something that was rightfully his. Shannon tried to resist his plundering lips, tried to pull her face away, but she couldn't think straight, couldn't clear the confusion fogging her mind. All she knew was the assault he was launching on her mouth, his lips commanding, his tongue playful yet deadly serious.

At last he released her, setting her back on her feet as he gazed down into her strangely unfocused eyes.

'Well?' he demanded softly.

Infuriated by the glint of triumph in his deep blue eyes, she managed to get herself back under some sort of control, though the rivers he'd sent surging through her body with his kisses were far from still.

'Mr Jacobsen,' she said, the words low and heavy with threat, 'if you ever try anything like that with me again I'll report you for sexual harassment so fast you won't know what's hit you. I'll let your fawning, adoring public know what you're really like behind that oh, so charming façade.' She rubbed the back of her hand over her mouth in a vain bid to obliterate the taste and touch of his lips still tingling on hers.

'Don't you think you're over-reacting, Miss Lea?' His voice was coldly mocking. 'I kissed you. Are you really so unaccustomed to a man's kisses?'

'You invaded my privacy,' she spat back at him. 'You simply did what you wanted to do with no thought or care as to how I should feel.'

'You feel pretty good,' he murmured appreciatively, and his words fuelled her anger still more.

'Go ahead,' she hissed. 'Treat it as a big joke. You obviously think you can do what you like with women, and perhaps that's the fault of those who've let you treat them this way in the past. But I warn you, Mr Jacobsen, you may be under the impression that you have some sort of droit de seigneur over make-up artists but, let me assure you, you're way off the mark. So if you value your anatomy, I suggest you keep your marauding Viking hands to yourself in the future.'

She turned her back on him then, and marched

over to the chair where her hold-all and jacket lay. Without so much as a backward glance she left the room, indignation clear in the rigidity of her spine as his mocking laugh rang out behind her.

Her temper fumed on unabated till she was well clear of the city, beginning to calm down only after she'd crossed the border into Scotland. Then slowly her sense of humour began to reassert itself and she was able to laugh, remembering the look of amazement on his handsome, hawklike face when she'd threatened to report him for sexual harassment. Little wonder he'd been amazed—Dane Jacobsen was probably more accustomed to having to fight adoring women off. To find one who was less than acquiescent must have been a considerable shock.

Her brows puckered thoughtfully as she ran through the scene in her mind again; maybe she had over-reacted. When push came to shove, all he'd really done was make a pass at her—it wasn't the first she'd had to deal with, and probably wouldn't be the last. In truth, she'd never reacted to male advances with such venom before—in fact she'd always prided herself on being able to stay cool. So why had she launched such a scathing verbal attack on the hapless Dane? She reached for the radio tuning-dial, giving a little snort of self-disgust at her own choice of adjective. Hapless? That wolf? Just as hapless as the plundering Norse overlord he'd been playing for the past few weeks!

She remembered the first time she'd seen him, striding tall and long-legged into the reception area of the TV station, instantly dominating the place by sheer presence alone. She'd known him instantly, of course—those vivid eyes and high, prominent cheek-bones were unmistakable. The receptionist had obviously recognised him too, had practically fallen over herself to bat her long dark eyelashes at him. Shannon had watched the encounter with interest, while remaining singularly unmoved herself. Oh, he was handsome all right, she'd even grant him sexy for those who liked their men tall, solid and apparently carved from granite. Fortunately she'd learnt at a very early age never to be taken in by good looks alone.

He hadn't actually done anything to inspire the receptionist's obvious and instant infatuation, Shannon recalled, but then, he probably never needed to. Men like him were born with charm, exuded sensuality as unthinkingly as they breathed in air. Noticing the way the young woman's eyes had glazed over with undisguised longing, while he appeared faintly bored with the proceedings, Shannon had mentally given thanks for the fact that she wasn't drawn to gorgeous, self-centred hunks like this one.

Humming absent-mindedly along with the music on the radio as she sped on through the night, Shannon pursed her lips thoughtfully. Attracted to the big ape she hadn't been, but she'd be an all-out liar if she tried to pretend she hadn't enjoyed his kisses. *Enjoyed, be damned! They knocked you clean out of your socks if you were big enough to admit it.* Shannon gave an involuntary little start as though someone had spoken the words aloud, then laughed self-consciously, realising she'd simply been hearing the voice of a conscience that was inclined to be over-zealous in its insistence on honesty.

'So I got a kick out of his kisses,' she said aloud with a touch of defiance. 'It's not a federal crime. I'm a young female animal—as far as I'm aware everything's in good working order. My response to him simply proved that.'

But even as she spoke she found herself wondering about the way she'd reacted to his kisses; if anyone should be well armed to protect themselves against the attractions of a man like Dane, she should. Heaven knew, she'd had the lessons drummed into her often enough as a child. And yet there had been a fleeting moment, as he'd held her tight in his arms, when she'd found herself longing to lower her defences, to give in to the unfamiliar forces driving through her body with his touch.

Kelly would just love that admission, she thought with a faint grin. Ever since they'd first become friends she'd been obsessed with Shannon's love-life, or rather the lack of it. Given half a chance she'd have taken on the job of finding a soul-mate for Shannon with all the crusading zeal of a missionary, since she was blissfully convinced that true happiness could be found only in a strong relationship such as the one she had.

'It's a waste, that's what it is,' she'd said only recently. 'You're twenty-seven, you're beautiful—oh, yes you are ——' she'd dismissed Shannon's laughing denial with the airy wave of a hand—and you should be sharing your life with some gorgeous hunk by now, not returning night after night to a cold and empty flat.'

'But I don't want to be sharing my life with anyone, gorgeous hunk or not,' Shannon had pointed out mildly, managing with an effort not to remind Kelly they'd been over this ground a hundred times before. 'And I don't return night after night to the flat—

largely thanks to the fact that I am footloose and fancy-free, I can follow my job wherever it takes me.'

'So you return to a cold and empty hotel room instead,' Kelly snorted in disgust. 'It's unnatural, Shae, that's what it is.'

'Nonsense. Just because you're inhumanly happy living with Tom doesn't mean the rest of the world has to be cosily paired off into couples.'

Kelly considered that. 'Maybe not,' she conceded at last. 'Maybe some people were born to fly solo. But you're not one of them, Shae—you're too warm, too full of life. And, though I don't think you realise it yourself, you're also full of love. You just haven't found a good use for it yet.'

Maybe if she confided in Kelly about her background, the other woman would be more understanding, Shannon thought ruefully. But, close as they were, that was the one subject she'd never felt able to broach. She'd seen scorn, and worse still pity, in too many faces already—she couldn't bear to see either repeated in Kelly's emerald-green eyes.

Reaching Blairgowrie, the small town nearest the slopes of Glenshee, Shannon stopped to collect the ski equipment she'd hired in advance, feeling patently ridiculous as she tried on the heavy boots for size.

'Don't worry, miss,' the young man on duty in the shop said with a sympathetic grin. 'You'll soon get accustomed to them.'

'I'll take your word for that!' She turned to sign for the gear, and ran her eye over the other signatures on the page.

'Hasn't my friend collected her gear yet?' she

queried. 'Her name's Kelly Adam. I had thought she'd be here before me.'

'Kelly Adam?' He looked doubtful. 'I don't remember anyone of that name coming in.'

Shannon smiled. 'You'd remember her. She's a gorgeous, tall, green-eyed brunette.'

He shook his head, laying one hand on his heart. 'No, ma'am, she definitely hasn't been here. I'd probably still be lying in a dazed heap in the corner if she had been—I'm a definite sucker for green eyes.'

'Then watch out! She should be in at any time now.'

The young man helped her carry her gear out to the car, stowing most of it away in the boot.

'So where are you and your green-eyed friend staying, then?' he asked. 'Somewhere in Blairgowrie?'

She shook her head. 'We've taken a cottage a couple of miles from the slopes.'

'Could turn out to be a good thing,' he said approvingly. 'I wouldn't be at all surprised if the road from here to the slopes is blocked by tomorrow morning.'

'Blocked?' She glanced at him in surprise. 'But there's hardly any snow here.'

He chuckled. 'Don't be misled by that! A couple of miles further on and you'll find yourself in a totally different world—a winter world. And the forecast for tonight is for much more snow.'

'But won't the snow-ploughs clear it?'

He gave her a slightly pitying look. 'This is obviously your first time here. The ploughs and gritters do their best, of course, but it's not at all uncommon for the elements to get the better of them for a little while. They always get through in the end, though.'

'I'm glad to hear it.' For the first time Shannon began to have second thoughts about the trip. What if she were to be stranded in the mountains—marooned by a blizzard? Then she gave a tiny shrug. She couldn't back out now—Kelly would never forgive her. Anyway, she really needed the break.

'There you go, then, miss.' The young man closed the boot of the car and handed her the keys. 'Have a good time. Don't go breaking any limbs.'

'I'll try not to.' She clambered into the driver's seat. 'When Kelly eventually gets here will you please tell her I've gone ahead? And tell her to get a move on!'

He gave a quick salute. 'Will do. Drive carefully, now.'

It was good advice, as she discovered just a few miles out of town when, as he'd predicted, she found herself in a very different environment. The roads were still relatively clear, but the fields and hillsides were pure, unremitting white. It was as though a white cloak had been thrown over the entire countryside, a cloak which gleamed beneath an enormous ghostly-white moon, robbing the night of its darkness. It would have been easy to drive without headlights, though she didn't attempt it. She was entranced by the shimmering purity of the snow, drawn by it, yet faintly intimidated at the same time, aware of her own lack of importance in the face of all this glory. Kelly would feel the same way, she realised, experiencing a little spurt of pleasure at the prospect of seeing her friend soon. . . What about Dane Jacobsen? How would he react to all this?

Shannon groaned, wondering where that errant

little thought had sprung from. She'd cast the infuriating Viking from her mind ages before—or so she'd believed. Now she realised he'd been hovering on the verges of her thoughts, just waiting for an opportunity to pounce. Damn the man, he had no place in her scheme of things. Not that he'd want one anyway. All his kind generally wanted was a quick flirtation, an acquiescent woman, and a no-strings parting the following morning.

He'd described her as 'an intriguing challenge', she remembered now with a frown. Well, that simply meant he'd temporarily grown tired of easy conquests; after all, women must fall to his golden charms like ripe apples from a tree. Little wonder he saw some fresh sport in the pursuit of someone like Shannon, who was single-mindedly determined to keep him at arm's length.

And yet. . .there had been a moment when Dane's undeniable magnetism had reached out to her, too, ensnaring her in its thrall just as surely as it captured every other female. The cast and crew of *The Viking* had been filming on location and, finding herself for once with little to do, she'd taken a break to watch the great Dane Jacobsen in action. The scene had called for him to stand on a cliff-top, surveying the land stretching out behind—land he and his marauding band had taken by force. He'd raised his arms in a gesture of possession, and, even though she'd known it was all part of a beautifully sculpted drama, Shannon had felt a thrill deep inside, as though she too were part of the kingdom the Viking had taken for his own.

Well, she rationalised now, the man was a consummate actor, and even she couldn't deny his talent. In those few minutes she'd simply been reacting to the mood he'd created so skilfully.

It was snowing when she reached the side-road marked on the map, and she heaved a sigh of relief when she spotted the dark shape of a cottage. The snow was mind-blowingly beautiful, but she'd be glad to get inside, happier still when Kelly arrived. Content as she generally was to be alone, this place had a distinctly solitary feel to it, and she'd be more secure in Kelly's extrovert company.

The cottage was a pretty little place, furnished for comfort rather than style, with the living-room dominated by a huge fireplace, two big old armchairs set companionably at either side. Further back sat a heavy wooden table, and on it she found a note from the building's owner, informing her that provisions had been left in the fridge, that there was an ample supply of coal and logs in the shed outside, and wishing her 'good snow and happy skiing'.

Exploring further, she found a tiny, well-equipped kitchen, and upstairs two small but comfortable bedrooms with big old-fashioned double beds, and a bathroom with shower-cabinet as well as bath. She turned on the tap and gave a whoop of delight as water cascaded forth, hot and plentiful. After the long drive a good soak was just what she needed, and it would help pass the time till Kelly arrived.

As it turned out she was in the bath when she heard the sounds of a car pulling up outside, swiftly followed by tapping on the door, and she jumped quickly from the water, pausing only to belt a towelling robe about her waist.

'Trust you to arrive just as I'm having a bath!' Shannon pulled the door open, her arms flung wide apart in exuberant welcome, but the broad smile froze on her lips as she found herself confronted by a tall, masculine figure. Win an increasing feeling of horror, her gaze slid slowly upwards to rest in stunned disbelief on the hawklike features and deep-sea eyes of Dane Jacobsen.

CHAPTER TWO

'WHAT in the name of all things wonderful are you doing here?'

Since she felt as though someone had physically kicked her in the stomach, it took Shannon a moment or two to get the words out.

He raised a sardonic eyebrow. 'I'm delighted you're so pleased to see me.'

'Pleased?' Her voice rose an octave on the single word. 'I'm astounded! When I get over that I shall doubtless be horrified.' She glowered at him suspiciously. 'What are you doing here? What have you done with Kelly?'

Amusement glimmered deep in his blue eyes. 'Are you expecting to hear I hijacked her en route and left her trussed up in a lay-by?'

'Nothing you did would surprise me,' she returned coldly. 'Mr Jacobsen, I'd be grateful if you'd stop playing the comedian and simply answer my questions.'

'Then let's not stand here freezing to death.' He reached out one hand to touch her damp hair. 'You've obviously just come out of a shower.'

For a moment the sheer gall of the man kept her frozen in place, then Shannon shook his hand away, her eyes shooting sparks of contempt as she glowered up at him.

'I'll thank you to keep your hands to yourself,' she snapped. 'You've already taken too many liberties with me, and I don't appreciate being touched by strangers.'

'Nor by anyone else, I suspect,' he murmured more to himself than her. His eyes narrowed challengingly. 'And tell me, Miss Lea, just what would you do about it if I did touch you? I don't believe screaming would help you much here.'

A cold hand clutched at her heart as she absorbed the truth of his words. They were miles from anywhere—no one would hear her scream, and she wouldn't stand an earthly chance if she tried to outrun him. Refusing to let him see any trace of fear in her eyes, she squared up to him, pride stiffening her spine.

'I'm not afraid of you,' she said resolutely.

A faint smile quirked the corners of his mouth. 'The little kitten has courage, it seems,' he murmured. 'Good.' Then, stretching out one hand, he pushed her very gently to one side and strode past her into the living-room. 'You may be prepared to catch pneumonia,' he said quietly, 'but I am not. Now, why don't you make me a nice cup of hot coffee, and we can sit down like two civilised adults and I'll explain everything?'

'Of all the damned cheek! Make your own blasted coffee!'

'Then you can lay a fire, which is what I was about to do,' he said with a flash of annoyance. 'Why didn't you do that when you first arrived? The place would be less like a fridge by now if you had.'

She looked away from his questioning eyes, aware of a tell-tale blush warming her face.

'I didn't know how,' she admitted sulkily.

Even though she wasn't looking at him, she knew

he was smiling scornfully, and the awareness made her clench her hands into fists. On top of everything else, to have him laughing at her! How dared he?

'Then let's revert to Plan A,' he suggested calmly. 'You make the coffee, I'll light the fire.' When she remained stubbornly in place he grabbed her abruptly by the elbow, and she started back in fright, her eyes widening in alarm. 'If, however, you persist in being damned awkward, I'll be quite happy to let you freeze your butt off—and you'll suffer before I will, since I'm wearing considerably more clothes.' He gazed down at her, his lips thinned to a narrow line. 'Furthermore, you'll be none the wiser about Kelly. Or don't you care what's happened to your friend?'

Shooting him a look of pure undisguised venom, she wrenched her elbow from his grasp, then went through to the kitchen, anger churning inside her like the waves of a storm-tossed sea. It stayed with her as she clattered cups and saucers on to a tray and slammed the fridge-door shut after taking out the milk. It was still darkening her brows when she marched back through to the living-room, her back ramrod-straight.

'No biscuits?' He was sitting in one of the big armchairs, and in the grate a fire was beginning to burn nicely. Shannon was pleased to welcome the warmth of the flames, but his easy success with a task she knew would have taken her hours irritated her still further and she shot him a withering look.

'I'm so terribly sorry, Mr Jacobsen,' she returned, her voice dripping sarcasm, 'Cook didn't get round to baking any cookies today. I really must reprimand her.'

'Isn't there any food in this place?' His narrowed eyes betrayed his impatience.

'As a matter of fact, there is. *My* food.'

'Then bring me some.'

Her mouth dropped open at his casual command. Not only did he invade her privacy, he had the gall to sit there and demand that she serve him!

'I will not.'

He shrugged. 'Have it your own way. I thought you were anxious to hear about your friend.'

'Oh, for goodness' sake! All right, I'll bring you something to eat in a minute, but tell me about Kelly first.'

'That's better.' He nodded with patronising approval, and she had to do battle with an urge to pick up the nearest heavy object and hurl it at his infuriating head. 'Sit down.'

Inwardly seething, she did as she was told, carefully tucking her dressing-gown about her legs.

'Wise move,' he murmured. 'Who knows? Food might not be all I'm hungry for.'

'Mr Jacobsen!'

He gave a wintry little smile. 'She telephoned the studio to say she wouldn't be able to make it this weekend.'

'What? Well, of all the——'

'She said you'd understand.' His tone was mildly reproving.

'Well, I don't.' She knew she sounded like a sulky little girl, but his news was a shattering disappointment. 'This trip was Kelly's idea in the first place.' She gazed down at the floor despondently. 'All this way for nothing.' Then she glanced up sharply. 'How on earth do you know about this?'

The blue eyes regarded her steadily. 'I was in Reception when she phoned, but the call couldn't be put through to you, as your line was engaged. I agreed to pass on the message as I was on my way to Make-up.'

Shannon absorbed his words in silence for a moment, then her eyes opened wide in shock as their meaning sank in.

'You took the message *before* I left the building?'

He nodded.

'Then why on earth didn't you tell me as soon as you saw me?' She shook her head, entirely thrown by what she was hearing. 'If I'd known Kelly couldn't come, I'd have cancelled my own trip.'

'That's what I assumed.' Dane leaned forwards to stir the fire and, even in her confused state of mind, Shannon couldn't help but notice the man's innate grace of movement. 'But you seemed to be looking forward to the break, so I decided not to disappoint you.'

'*You* decided?' Anger bubbled up inside her like a geyser set to gush, and she made a valiant effort to hold it in check. She was determined not to lose her temper, at least until she'd got to the bottom of the riddle, but his apparent attempt at playing God with her life infuriated her. 'Look,' she said steadily, 'don't you understand? If you'd told me this in the make-up room when you came to have your hair cut, you'd have saved yourself a needless journey. There was no need at all for you to follow me here.'

He shrugged nonchalantly. 'A weekend's skiing suddenly seemed like a nice idea.'

'*Wha – at*?' She all but shrieked the word. 'But you can't stay here! It's completely out of the question.'

'Why? There are two bedrooms.'

'Yes, there arc, but——'

'Then there's no problem,' he cut in smoothly. 'We can be perfectly respectable and above board.'

'But we can't spend the weekend together.'

'Why not?' He eyed her with mild amusement.

'We don't even know each other.' In the face of his calm determination, Shannon was scrabbling wildly for plausible excuses.

'This is as good a way to get to know each other of any I can think of.' He raised one eyebrow mockingly. 'Just think, Miss Lea—we might even find we become friends.'

The very notion of becoming friendly with this arrogant, pig-headed latter-day Viking would have made her laugh if the situation hadn't been so horribly unfunny. As it was, the prospect of spending so much time in his company was enough to send cold shivers down her spine. She wouldn't do it—wouldn't allow him to railroad her into something she had absolutely no desire for.

She slid him a sideways glance, wondering how he'd react if she announced she was leaving immediately. Instinct told her not to bother. Having taken the trouble to travel all this way in the first place, he'd doubtless find some means of coercing her to stay.

She gave a little shrug, intended to convey reluctant acceptance of the situation. 'I'll go and see about fixing a meal.'

'Good. I'll bring my luggage in from the car.'

The irony of the situation hit her as she began preparing a meal from the provisions she'd brought with her. Here she was, all alone in the wildly romantic snow-covered Scottish mountains with a man most women would give their eye-teeth simply to be in the same room with, and her only wish was to get away from him. She could just imagine Kelly's horror if she knew.

'This is all your fault, Kelly Adam,' she muttered, savagely stirring a panful of soup. 'If I didn't know it was impossible, I'd swear you'd cooked up this little plot deliberately.'

The more she thought about the situation she'd somehow landed in, the more determined she became to get out of it. But how? She was sure Dane would try to prevent her leaving, and there was no way she could ever hope to beat such a formidable opponent. Her only option would be to employ guile, and steal away when he was unaware of it. When he went to bed, that would be the best time.

With a little effort she managed to be reasonably amiable throughout supper, even refraining from a caustic retort when he complimented her cooking. Since the meal had come entirely from tins, she could hardly believe he was being sincere, but she merely smiled and nodded her thanks.

'That's better, Shannon.' He leaned back in his chair pushing his empty plate away from him. 'It's not really so hard to be pleasant, is it?'

'I don't believe I've ever been unpleasant,' she returned, noting his easy use of her Christian name. So he thought they were about to become friends, did he? He'd realise the truth when he discovered her empty bed in the morning. The thought sent a mischievous little smile to her lips, and he raised his eyebrows quizzically.

'Not unpleasant, perhaps,' he said thoughtfully, 'but you haven't exactly gone out of your way to make me feel welcome—either here or back at the television studio.'

'My job is to make people look good,' she replied a little tartly. 'It doesn't say anywhere in my contract I have to make them feel good, too.'

'But doesn't it make things more enjoyable if you can befriend the people you're working with?' The deep-sea eyes never wavered as he gazed directly at her, and she had to force herself not to turn away, aware of the strangest feeling that he could somehow see straight into her mind.

'In my occupation the people you meet tend to be here one day and gone the next—or I am, since I work freelance. That doesn't exactly allow much chance to form lasting relationships.'

'Does that ever bother you?'

She shot him a curious glance. 'Why should it?'

'I'd have thought it could be a pretty lonely existence.' He fingered his chin thoughtfully. 'Don't you get lonely?'

Unthinkingly she nodded, then scowled darkly, annoyed at herself. 'I'd have thought the same thing would apply to you,' she said, evading a direct answer. 'You work all over the place, and you must spend a great deal of time away from home.'

He nodded. 'I do.'

She waited for him to elaborate, but when he remained silent her forehead creased in an irritated frown. 'I suppose the great Dane Jacobsen never has to search for willing company. People probably fall over themselves to be with you—at least, if the newspapers are anything to go by.'

His eyes darkened dangerously. 'What do you mean by that?'

She looked away, made uneasy by the threatening expression on his harsh features. Why on earth had she risked provoking him? 'Only that you seem to be the darling of the tabloids,' she muttered. 'Every time you're photographed you have another blonde lovely on your arm.'

She could feel the heat of his glare even though she wasn't looking at him. 'The "great Dane Jacobsen" is only a human being, and would never claim to be anything else,' he said curtly. 'There are those who want to be seen with me simply because of who I am. Are you condemning *me* for that?'

She shifted uncomfortably in her seat. 'No, but. . .'

'Or are you guilty of inverted snobbery?'

The question made her flinch. 'I don't know what you mean.'

'I mean—have you been avoiding me like the very plague simply because of who I am?'

She opened her mouth to answer, then closed it again. Put on the spot like that she wasn't honestly sure of the true response. *Had* she been avoiding him because he was famous? Then she shook her head. It was a ridiculous suggestion—she wasn't as shallow as that. 'I meet famous people practically every day. I make no attempt to avoid them.'

'Who's the most famous person you've ever met?' His eyes challenged her to answer honestly.

She considered the question, running a checklist through her mind. At last she glanced up, tilting her chin in unconscious defiance. 'You are.'

His lips quirked in satisfaction. 'I think I rest my case, m'lud.'

'Would you care for coffee?' Shannon stood up

abruptly, suddenly desperate to be away from those penetrating eyes.

'Sit down. We haven't finished this conversation.'

'Conversation?' She sent him a withering look. 'It seems more like an interrogation to me, and frankly I don't enjoy being quizzed like this. By rights I should be sitting here with Kelly enjoying a cosy chat, not shielding myself from verbal arrows.'

'So stop shielding yourself,' he retorted swiftly. 'Let some of those barriers down, Shannon Lea. What harm could it do?'

For a long moment she gazed back at him, feeling an inexplicable and totally uncharacteristic desire to do just that. Then she stiffened her spine. The man's charm and persuasive ways were legendary. She wasn't about to become the latest victim in a long line to fall under his spell. 'I'm going to clear these plates away, then I'm going to bed, *Mr* Jacobsen,' she said with quiet resolution. 'Perhaps you'd be good enough to make sure the fire's safe before you turn in? I've taken the bedroom on the right-hand side at the top of the stairs. I trust you'll find the other one to your satisfaction, though I fear it's hardly up to the five-star standards you're doubtless accustomed to.'

He made no reply, but she saw the glint of amusement in his eyes and turned away, her lips tightening in annoyance. This man was lodging himself like an irritating burr under her skin. The faster she got away from him the better, for her sanity if nothing else.

In the safe solitude of her bedroom, Shannon quickly stripped off her dressing-gown and pulled on the lightweight jogging-pants and sweatshirt she'd travelled in. Fortunately she hadn't finished unloading the car, so would only have a single hold-all to carry back downstairs. He was welcome to the food in the pantry, she thought grimly, resisting the temptation to hope it choked him. She cast a regretful look at the big double bed with its luxurious continental quilt. Weary already from the long drive north, she'd have given almost anything to simply fold herself into its comfortable depths and fall asleep. But this could be her only chance to get away. She didn't dare mess it up.

Afraid she might doze off if she gave in to temptation and lay down on the bed, she sat down instead on the room's only chair, and picked up a book, absorbing not a single word as she waited for the sounds that would mean he was turning in for the night. At last she heard the creak of footsteps on the stairs, and hardly dared breathe until he closed his own room door. If he'd decided to look in, and seen her fully dressed, the game would have been up.

Stifling her impatience, Shannon waited another half-hour, then, moving with as much stealth as she could muster, pulled on a jacket, slung the hold-all over her shoulder, and tiptoed quietly towards the door. Slowly she eased it open, offering up a silent thanks as it slid noiselessly over the carpet, then made her way one careful step at a time downstairs. The last step but one creaked protestingly and she grimaced apprehensively, her body almost turning to stone as she waited for Dane to suddenly appear and demand to know what she was doing. When there were no sounds of activity she heaved a great sigh of relief and carried on through the living-room towards the front door.

Outside the snow was still falling, thicker than ever now, the flakes large and white. It was hard to walk without making a crunching sound, but she did her best, relaxing only when she reached her car and slid carefully into the driver's seat. He'd hear the engine starting, of course, but, by the time he'd got himself together enough to do anything about it, she should at least have a head start. Anyway, there was no real reason to suppose he'd come chasing after her. He might be annoyed for a moment to find his prey had fled, but there was nothing to stop him simply making the best of a bad job and having a weekend's skiing. Doubtless he'd be able to find much more amenable company on the slopes tomorrow morning. She was faintly perplexed to discover the thought brought no pleasure.

Easing the car into first gear, she set off back along the road, a frown deepening on her face as she was forced to crawl along at a snail's pace, unable to see more than a couple of feet ahead in the ever-thickening snow. For the first time she began to wonder if she'd been foolhardy—no matter how strong her desire to get away, she shouldn't have put her own safety at risk. Now here she was, in the middle of the night, miles from anywhere but the cottage, and in a virtual white-out. If conditions didn't improve soon she'd be in very real danger of getting stuck in the snow—as it was she couldn't have said with any real certainty whether she was driving on the road or in a field.

'All this because you were so all-fired determined to get away from Dane,' she muttered savagely, peering through a snow-clogged windscreen. Her desperation to flee seemed faintly ridiculous now, but she stiffened her failing resolve with the reminder that he had tracked her to Glenshee, giving her no say whatsoever in the matter. She'd felt like a trapped animal back in the cottage, and like a trapped animal her only instinct had been to escape. Ironically it seemed now that flight had placed her in far greater danger than staying put could ever have done.

'Sweet heaven,' she whispered to the empty car, 'please let me reach the main road safely. Surely it will be clearer than this?'

When the car suddenly collided with something solid she knew her prayers hadn't been answered. Since she'd been wearing her seatbelt and travelling at a very slow speed, she wasn't hurt, but the shock was enough to make her tremble. For long moments she simply sat, as if waiting for someone to tell her what to do, her own power of reasoning immobilised. Then, realising she was on the verge of helpless tears, she made a valiant effort to pull herself together.

'Get out and see what you've hit, Shae,' she told herself grimly. 'If it's nothing major you might still be able to carry on.'

What she'd hit or, more accurately, ploughed into, was a thick snowdrift, piled across the road. One glance was enough, even through the swirling flakes, to tell Shannon she was well and truly stuck. Even as she watched, the snow was beginning to cover the car. There was only one thing she could do, though everything within her rebelled against it. She'd have to return to the cottage. Uttering a vivid stream of oaths, most of them directed at Dane, she turned back, forced to drop her head forwards against the driving force of the snow.

She could only have driven about a mile, she estimated, but as she trudged back along the road it seemed like a marathon trek. Within seconds she was shivering, her lightweight clothing no protection against the bitingly chill wind, her hands and feet quickly becoming numb in the icy cold. Hearing the noise of a car's engine, she looked up to see approaching headlights, and a feeling of dread, colder even than the snow, settled over her like a heavy cloak. The car slowed to a halt before her, and Dane jumped from the driver's seat, his features darkly contorted with anger.

'What the hell do you think you're playing at?' His voice was blisteringly harsh. 'Are you trying to kill yourself?'

With an effort Shannon pulled herself up to her full five-feet-three-inch height, desperately striving for some sort of dignity, even though she was shivering all over.

'What does it look like I'm doing?' she demanded. 'I'm trying to get away from you!'

'You stupid little fool,' he shot back viciously. 'Don't you know how treacherous conditions can be on the Scottish mountains in the middle of winter? Didn't you even stop to consider that, before you set off for an evening drive?' He shook his head in angry bewilderment, then, in one swift easy movement, bent to hook his arm beneath her knees.

'What do you think you're doing?' Her eyes flew wide open in surprise as he lifted her easily into his arms.

'What I'd like to be doing is putting you over my knee and giving you the spanking you heartily deserve,' he said grimly.

'If you lay one hand on me. . .' She tried to pull away from him, but he held her effortlessly, unmoved by her struggles.

'Be quiet, Shannon,' he said through gritted teeth. 'You've brought me very close to the end of my patience. Don't push me any further.'

Held captive in his powerful arms, she glared at him mutinously. Everything within her wanted to fight him, but the forbidding expression on his harsh features, and the unmistakable threat in his voice, told her in no uncertain manner she'd regret it if she did.

'I don't see any need for the caveman act,' she said stiffly. 'I'm not an infant. I don't need to be carried.'

'Don't tempt me to tell you what you do need, lady,' he shot back. 'It might be more than your delicate ears could stand. I'm carrying you because you need to get back into the warmth as fast as possible, and this is quicker than letting you walk by yourself.'

'Then why don't we simply drive back? Your car isn't stuck.'

'No, it isn't,' he returned curtly. 'But would you care to tell me how I could turn it round, since the snow's narrowed the width of the road to a single track? And don't suggest I try reversing all the way, since I have no intention of landing in a ditch and immobilising both vehicles.'

Carrying her as easily as if she were made of feathers, Dane strode out towards the cottage. Shannon knew she should be grateful to him for leaving his warm bed to rescue her from what could have been a perilous situation, but, clasped in his arms like this, she felt both rebellious and faintly ridiculous. Knowing he was in the right, that she had taken a stupid risk, only made things worse.

In the cottage he dumped her none too gently in one of the armchairs before the fire, pausing only to stir the embers back to life before stamping out towards the kitchen. Suddenly swamped by exhaustion, she slumped back against the cushions and closed her eyes, reliving the awful moment when the car had slid into the snowdrift. Then her eyes flew open as she felt her sodden shoes being pulled off and her feet engulfed in large, warm hands.

'What are you doing?'

'Trying to ensure you don't get frostbite, though lord knows you deserve it.' He tossed his head disgustedly. 'Look at these things—training shoes! In a blizzard! If you'd been out there much longer, God knows what might have happened.'

'If it weren't for you I'd never have been out there in the first place.' She tried to tug her foot free, but he held it easily, his strong, capable fingers massaging her frozen toes, making her groan as they came slowly back to life.

'Don't lay the blame for this crazy stunt on me, lady,' he retorted. 'You're the one who tried to get herself killed out there!'

'I'd have been all right if I'd made it to the main road.'

'It's probably just as well for you that you didn't,' he returned curtly. 'The snow-ploughs won't be out till early morning, and if you'd got stuck in the middle of nowhere. . .' He let the sentence hang unfinished, and she shivered, struck anew by the danger she'd voluntarily placed herself in. 'People like you shouldn't be allowed anywhere near the mountains, and especially not in winter,' he said with sudden savagery. 'You have no understanding of the conditions, no idea of the way things can change in a flash.'

'And you do?' Flayed by his voice, she tilted her chin defiantly, attempting to look as though his scorn meant nothing to her, though in truth it cut deeper than knives.

'I've lived in the mountains,' he said grimly. 'I've seen what can happen to fools. I've also seen what can happen to the poor brave souls who risk their own lives searching for them.' He eyed her contemptuously. 'I suppose you're like all the rest—a city-kid who's never been away from the busy streets before.'

The irony of that was almost enough to make Shannon laugh out loud. He couldn't be much further from the truth—but, even as she opened her mouth to tell him so, some deep-down instinct stopped her in her tracks. It was clear he already thought her beneath contempt and, if she was truthful with herself, that was a painful fact to accept. She wasn't about to give him any further ammunition.

Obviously taking her silence for agreement, he gave a little snort of disgust. 'Here, drink this.'

'What is it?' She took the mug he was holding out to her, eyeing its contents suspiciously.

'Frankly, I wish it were hemlock, but it's brandy.' He sat back on his heels, his eyes raking over her with hostile curiosity. 'All right, Shannon Lea, I want some answers from you now—and I want the truth. Why did you do it?'

She dropped her eyes to the mug, unable to face his withering scorn.

'You should never have come here,' she muttered.

'Lady, if I'd known I was dealing with a certifiable lunatic wild horses wouldn't have dragged me here.'

'So why did you come?' His words goaded her own temper to life. 'Nobody asked you to.'

He laughed mirthlessly. 'I wish to God I knew. Maybe I just wanted to discover if there really was a flesh-and-blood woman beneath that starched exterior.'

'In other words you couldn't bear the thought that there might just be one female in a hundred-mile radius who didn't fall apart at the seams every time you deigned to smile in her direction,' she spat back. 'You couldn't believe there might be just one woman impervious to your world-famous charms.' His eyes narrowed dangerously, but she ploughed on regardless, too wound up now to pay any attention to the threat. 'Isn't that the truth, Dane Jacobsen? You saw me as a challenge—a little harder than the rest, perhaps, but there for the taking, nevertheless. Ultimately just another conquest to lump in with the rest, so your score-sheet could remain unblemished by failure.'

'Oh, no.' He let the foot he'd been massaging fall to the floor with a thud, and she winced. 'I'd never make the mistake of assuming you were like other women—because they have blood running in their veins, warm, human, fallible blood. You, lady, have nothing but iced water.'

She flinched, cut by the whiplash of his words.

'You know nothing about me,' she snapped. 'Nothing at all.'

He nodded slowly. 'You're right. But perhaps my real mistake lay in assuming there was something there to know—something more than a cardboard cut-out.' He rose to his feet, towering over her. 'Well, I know better now. Go to bed, Shannon Lea. I'll be gone by the time you wake up in the morning. Then perhaps you'll be happy—all alone in a kingdom of ice.' His eyes darkened derisively. 'And I can't think of a more appropriate place for you.'

Shannon stood up, laying her empty mug on the mantelpiece. The brandy and the fire had done their work, now physically, at least, she was warm again. But there was a numb place deep inside, a place he'd created with his cruelly scathing words, and she gazed back at him with something near loathing as he walked away towards the stairs. At the last minute he turned back.

'You'd better sleep in my bed.'

'What?' She felt a returning surge of anger—after all that had been said, did he really think she would sleep with him?

His wintry smile failed to reach his eyes. 'Don't panic. I wasn't suggesting you betray any human warmth in your soul by sharing a bed—simply pointing out that yours is unslept in, whereas mine at least should still have a remnant of heat in it.'

'That really isn't necessary,' she returned coolly, though her pale cheeks flamed at the thought of lying where he had lain.

He gave her a look that brooked no further arguments. 'Don't annoy me any more tonight, Shannon,' he said in a voice that was soft yet laden with threat. 'For once in your life, just do as you're told.'

Even as she turned towards the staircase she was still trying to come up with a good reason for not sleeping in his bed, but when she reached the top step she turned with a resigned sigh towards his room, too bone weary to argue any more. And, she was forced to admit as she climbed between the still-warm sheets, his bed was considerably more appealing than the cold one in her room. She snuggled down beneath the duvet, desperately trying not to think that just a short while ago it had been wrapped round his powerful body, but as she turned her face into the pillow she was all but overwhelmed by the scent of him—a clean, heady, masculine smell that owed nothing to any kind of artificial fragrance. Lying there in his bed, she was suddenly beset by wild, crazy images of lying there in his arms, and, even as she tried to block them out, her body grew warm with the memory of the moment when he'd kissed her in the make-up room.

'For goodness' sake, Shae,' she muttered into the darkness, 'you're no better than the rest of them—you're being betrayed by a longing that's nothing more than physical.' That road led only to self-destruction—she should know that better than anyone . . .only had to conjure up the sad, embittered look in her mother's hazel eyes to realise the depths of pain such an entanglement could cause.

Even now, of course, her mother would deny that she'd been driven by physical needs—she still insisted on living the lie that hers had been a love-story doomed to disaster. Shannon had never been able to believe that; as a child she'd seen a photograph of her father, and even then she'd been stunned to silence by his incredible good looks. As she grew older she came slowly to understand how a sensible, level-headed woman like her mother could have her head completely turned by unaccustomed glamour. But with understanding had come a growing determination that she would never fall into the same trap—would never allow herself to be ruled by a foolish, hoping heart.

Despairingly she thumped the pillows into a more comfortable shape, as though she could vent her frustration on them. Even with all she knew, the feelings invading her body as she lay in Dane's bed were totally alien—she had no idea how to handle them, let alone get rid of them. But it hardly mattered. Tomorrow he'd be gone, and this whole crazy charade would be over, once and for all.

CHAPTER THREE

SHANNON slept badly that night, haunted by dreams of great swirling snowflakes and a hawk-faced man who loomed out of the deadly white mass with fury in his eyes. The restlessness showed in her face, she realised despondently, looking at her own pale-faced reflection the following morning, and remembering that her entire collection of cosmetics was still stowed in the stranded car. Ironically she rarely used much make-up herself, but right now she could have done with a cover-up stick to hide the dark shadows beneath her eyes and some blusher to conceal at least a little of her pallor.

She did what she could with her tousled mass of auburn curls, but when she twisted it into its usual topknot the starkness of the style served only to emphasise the weariness in her wide-set eyes, and with a little mutter of disgust she let the curls fall again, tumbling about her shoulders in riotous abandon. It really would be very much more practical to have her hair cut, she told herself severely for the umpteenth time, but the simple truth was that she liked having her hair long, loved the feeling of the heavy silken strands on her skin.

With a last dissatisfied glance in the mirror, she left the bedroom and made her way downstairs, vaguely wondering why she didn't feel light of heart. Dane was gone—he'd made that promise the night before, and for some reason she felt sure he was, despite all, a man of his word. Now the choice was hers—she could stay on in the cottage for the weekend as planned, or she could cut her losses and head for home. Well, there was no need to decide straight away; she could think about it over a leisurely solo breakfast.

She walked into the kitchen, humming tunelessly under her breath, only to stop in her tracks at the sight of Dane standing at the cooker. Dressed in a pair of faded old jeans and a warm cotton shirt that strained to contain the body it covered, he was clearly quite at home in his role as chef, and for a moment she watched, strangely drawn by the sight of him in this unexpected setting. She'd never have suspected the Viking of possessing culinary skills. Then she remembered he wasn't even supposed to be there, and the faint smile playing about her lips vanished.

'I thought I could trust you,' she said accusingly.

'Good morning to you, too!' To her further chagrin he didn't even raise his eyes from his task.

'You said you'd be gone by the time I got up.' She bit her lip, hating the shrewish sound of her own voice. Dammit, why did the man have this effect on her?

'And I meant it.' He slid her a sardonic sideways glance. 'However, the weather-gods had different ideas.'

'What do you mean?'

'I mean, Miss Shannon Lea, that it's been snowing heavily all night long. The roads are still blocked.'

'Oh.' She looked down at the floor, unconsciously scuffing the wooden boards with one foot. 'When will they be clear?'

He shrugged. 'There's no way of telling.'

'Then we're stuck here? Together?'

His answering smile was coldly mocking. 'It would seem that way, yes.'

She was momentarily lost for words, thrown completely off balance by this new turn of events. She'd been so sure she'd be alone again this morning, and to have him still here under the same roof, calmly cooking breakfast, was almost more than she could cope with. Her eyes narrowed as a sudden dart of suspicion struck home.

'How do you know the roads are still blocked?'

He glanced at her disgustedly. 'If they weren't, I'd be a good many miles away by now. Do you honestly think your company's so scintillating that I want to spend still more time in it?'

'Scintillating enough for you to drive all the way to Glenshee,' she retorted swiftly.

A muscle twitched in his cheek, and she waited in slight apprehension for an acid rejoinder, but he merely nodded towards the radio on the kitchen dresser. 'I've been tuned in to the local station,' he said shortly. 'It gives regular reports on the state of the roads.'

'I see.' Feeling faintly uncomfortable, Shannon moved towards the pantry to fetch a cup and saucer. Finding him here had robbed her of her appetite, but she needed a coffee badly. Cup in hand, she was about to sit opposite him at the small kitchen table, but the unwelcoming look in his deep blue eyes changed her mind, and she wandered aimlessly through to the living-room.

Lord, what a nightmare this was! She should have been sharing breakfast with Kelly right now, laughing and chatting, catching up on all that had been happening over the past few months. Instead she was holed up for goodness knew how long with a man who clearly despised her—and not without reason, she admitted silently, leaning her forehead against the cold glass of the window. Her stunt of last night had been infantile, to say the least, if not positively life-threatening. In truth, she should be grateful to him for coming to her rescue—instead she could barely bring herself to be civil.

She was still there some time later, gazing sightlessly through the glass over the snow-covered fields beyond, when she felt a strange tingle in the back of her neck, and knew he was standing behind her. She turned quickly, rattled by his presence.

'I was just looking at the scenery.' To her immense irritation she found herself babbling, as though there was some need for her to explain herself to him. 'It's really beautiful, isn't it? Such a shame to come all the way here and then miss out on skiing.'

He seemed faintly bored as he gazed over her head through the window. Then he shrugged. 'I don't intend to miss out on anything.'

She bridled at the apparent underlying threat in his words.

'Just what is that supposed to mean?'

The blue eyes bored into her for a long moment, and she fought the urge to look away from his coldly penetrating look.

'I mean, Miss Shannon Lea,' he said with exaggerated patience, 'that there's plenty of snow for the taking right outside this cottage. What did you think I meant?'

Flustered anew, she felt a warm flush of embarrassment flood her face as she searched vainly for an answer.

'Surely you didn't think I was referring in any way to you?' His voice was openly mocking now, his expression derisive.

'Well, of course not, but. . .'

'Even now you still believe your body to be so irresistible that I must be hungering for it?' The notion clearly amused him, and anger overcame Shannon's awkwardness as she glared back at him.

'Frankly, Mr Jacobsen, I wouldn't put anything past you. I don't believe any such nonsense about myself, but I do believe your ego is so invincible that you're incapable of believing any woman could be totally uninterested in sleeping with you. Well, let me tell you—you've just found one who is.'

His lips twisted savagely. 'Lady, I'd rather sleep with a nestful of vipers, though frankly I'm not sure I'd be able to tell the difference.' He turned on his heel then, thudding his coffee-cup down on the table as he strode towards the front door. When it slammed behind him she let out a long, shaky breath and felt blindly for a chair, afraid she'd collapse without some means of support.

He'd done it again—made her lose her temper all over again, and she couldn't even understand why. She'd always known she possessed a temper, of course; but, after one horribly painful childhood incident that was still burned into her memory like a scar, she'd fought hard to master it, refusing ever again to let anger get the better of her. Until Dane Jacobsen had barged into her life she'd done pretty well, too, she thought darkly—but he had a peculiar knack of stripping away those carefully constructed defences, to reveal the real emotions underneath.

It could all have been so different. A faint, ironic

smile played about her mouth as she allowed herself, just for a minute, to imagine what the weekend could have held if she had been one of Dane's legion of devoted followers. She was actually living through the kind of situation fantasies were made of—stranded in the snow with one of the world's great sex symbols—and all she could do was argue with him.

Yet she already knew, to her cost, that she wasn't totally immune. She shuddered, remembering his deeply thrilling kisses and the way they'd made her feel, even though everything within her rebelled against his easy command. What would it feel like to go further than just kissing? she wondered hazily. What would it feel like to abandon herself to his touch?

Shannon dropped her head into her hands, raking her fingers through her hair as though they could strip her mind of its suddenly restless, feverish thoughts. Dear lord, what was she doing? Even to allow such images into her mind meant she'd dropped the barriers too far—something she couldn't afford to do if she wanted to survive this experience mentally intact.

The imagination was a powerful beast; left unchecked it could overwhelm every other good sense a person possessed. . .which was exactly what had happened to her mother, she reminded herself forcibly. She'd imagined herself deeply in love with a man who'd spun her impossible yarns of riches and position, only to abandon her in the end to shame and ridicule.

She, Shannon Lea, was the living result of that, so she should be better armed than most against the lure of the glamorous. It was painful to realise that, even with all she knew, she still wasn't completely safe from the betraying needs of her own foolish body.

An hour later she was once again despondently staring through the window, completely at a loss for anything to do. She'd tried to read, but her attention kept being drawn to what was happening outside and, even though she was annoyed at herself for giving in so easily, she kept returning to watch Dane's powerful figure swishing expertly across the snow. Even to her inexperienced eyes it was clear he was no beginner, and frankly it was a pleasure to watch him. There was just enough slope in the field to give him a decent run, though she felt sure it must be frustrating for someone so skilled to be stuck on what was little better than a nursery area.

Turning away for the umpteenth time, she gave a little frustrated sigh. She could have had fun out there with Kelly, even though neither of them had ever been on skis before. Instead she was stuck in the house like a sulky schoolgirl sentenced to after-hours detention. Then again, it was only her own stubbornness that was keeping her indoors, she acknowledged glumly. Dane didn't own the fields; there was no real reason why she shouldn't go out and play in the snow, too.

The thought lit a mischievous little spark deep within, and at first she shook her head, telling herself it was a ridiculous idea. But the notion, once born, firmly took root, refusing to let her settle, and as she wandered aimlessly about the living-room she realised she'd soon be in danger of going stir-crazy if she had to look at the same four walls much longer. And it was a lovely day—cold but clear, the sky a vast, beautiful blue.

Minutes later she was in her bedroom, hurriedly changing into the black salopettes she'd bought on Kelly's instruction, adding a warm sweater and matching black ski-jacket. She grimaced a little as she caught sight of her own reflection in the full-length mirror. The outfit was practical, but hardly stylish—far removed from the kind of slick designer gear Dane would doubtless favour. Shannon hadn't looked closely at what he was wearing, but it was a fair bet he'd choose the kind of ski-clothes favoured in the jet-set resorts. In her present sensitive frame of mind she didn't feel up to looking like the poor relation beside him, but then, she had no intention of going anywhere near him. There was plenty of room out there for them both, after all.

To her chagrin he skied straight over to her as soon as she reached the field, and a faint, self-mocking grin touched her lips as she surveyed his outfit close at hand. Wrong again. His ski-gear was well-worn, respectable—and perfectly ordinary, without a designer label in sight.

'Something wrong?' he enquired levelly.

'Not at all.' She let her eyes sweep over him, reluctantly impressed at the way his magnificent physique still managed to display itself even under the bulky quilted trousers and jacket. 'Saving the expensive gear for St Moritz, are we? Isn't Glenshee good enough for *haute couture*?'

His eyes narrowed dangerously at the undisguised sarcasm in her voice

'What makes you think I even possess such clothes?'

She shrugged nonchalantly, feeling a little uncomfortable under his hard stare.

'You're an actor, aren't you?'

'And that automatically makes me a fully paid-up member of the jet-set?'

'Doesn't it?' Nettled by his tone, Shannon glared defensively back at him, belatedly wishing she'd never got into yet another argument she hadn't a hope of winning. She'd been in his company for less than a minute, and already they were sparring.

A faint, derisive smile curved Dane's lips as he slowly shook his head. 'You really are a little snob, aren't you?'

'I'm *what*?' She was cut to the quick by the accusation. 'Don't be ridiculous. I'm a nobody—in material terms I possess next to nothing of any monetary value. How could I possibly be a snob?'

He was clearly amused by her reaction, his eyes slanting into a lazy, mocking smile that somehow rattled her more than his anger had done.

'In my experience snobbishness doesn't equate with position, power or possessions. In fact, it's quite often the reverse. Those who are highest on the social ladder can be the most open-minded.'

'And you'd doubtless know all about that,' she retorted, unable to keep an edge of bitterness from her voice. 'The acting fraternity generally seem to have free entry to those circles.'

'"Those circles"?' he echoed. '"The acting fraternity"? Have you ever listened closely to yourself, Shannon? Are you aware of placing labels on people, or is it something you do unthinkingly—automatically?'

'I don't,' she muttered ungraciously.

'But you do.' He nodded slowly. 'And I think that's why you dislike me. I am an actor. It seems you have me weighed up, categorised and pigeon-holed all on the basis of the job I do.'

'My opinion of you has nothing to do with your profession.' she returned hotly. 'But I refuse to be one of your doting cavalcade of admirers.'

'"Methinks the lady doth protest too much",' he quoted softly, a strange gleam in his vivid blue eyes. 'Is that it, Shannon? Are you waiting for me to simply sweep away all your maidenly protests? If I remember correctly, the woman I held in my arms back in that little make-up room didn't put up more than a token fight.' He came closer still, and she backed away only to be halted in her tracks by the wooden fence behind her. 'Is that the answer? Should I simply ignore what that delicious mouth is saying, and remember instead how sweet it tastes and how it can mould so beautifully to mine?'

To her horror, his words set off a ripple of excitement within her, and she felt a betraying warmth flood her cheeks.

'You really are incredible,' she said with all the venom she could muster. 'You're so damn full of your own importance you can't get it into your thick skull that the world wasn't created solely for your amusement. You might have thought I'd happily become a little playmate for you to while away a few tedious hours with, but let me tell you, Mr Jacobsen, you were way off the mark.'

Throwing him a look of haughty disdain, she bent down to push her boots into the ski-bindings, furiously aware that he was watching her every move.

'What are you doing?' he asked mildly.

'What does it look like I'm doing?' She straightened up, forced to make a quick grab for the gate as the skis threatened to slide away with her. Trying to look as dignified as she could, under the circumstances, she looked him straight in the eyes, with more than a touch of defiance. 'I'm going to do what I came here to do in the first place. Ski.'

He nodded. 'Have you done much skiing?'

It was the condescending look on his face that did it. Even as she heard her own voice she was horrified by what it was saying, but somehow couldn't stop herself, even though it went completely against the grain to tell such blatant lies.

'Masses,' she returned blithely. 'After all, I was born and brought up in the north of Scotland. Children there learn to ski practically before they can walk.' Which in itself was no lie, but it just so happened that she'd never been allowed to join the other children in such frivolous pastimes, she reflected with a touch of resentment.

'Good. Then you won't need me to teach you.'

'Teach me?' She sent him an incredulous look. 'Certainly not. I can manage perfectly well on my own.'

'Come on, then. Let's get skiing.'

As he moved away, Shannon sent a silent stream of curses after the mischievous imp in her soul which had landed her in this, desperately trying to remember the instructions she'd skimmed through in the beginners' 'learn-to-ski' handbook Kelly had given her. The snag was, everything had seemed perfectly fine and reasonable written down in black and white—but the book had omitted to mention that on snow the skis took on a life all of their own. As she tentatively slid one ski forwards half an inch, the other decided it would rather proceed in a sideways direction, and, with a strangled squawk, she hit the deck, an ungainly tangle of arms, legs and ski-sticks.

'Having problems down there?' Dane's expression was infuriatingly bland as he glanced down at her, and Shannon glared back at him, all too aware of just how ridiculous she must look.

'I hit a rock, that's all.'

He nodded gravely. 'Of course.'

'Look——' now she was finding it all but impossible to get back to her feet, and the embarrassment of having him witness her futile struggles was fast becoming unbearable '—I'm quite happy just to potter about by myself here; you really don't have to hang around me.'

'I don't mind.' His lips twitched in amusement.

'Will you please go away?' The plea was heartfelt, but the tone of her voice made it into a peremptory command, and his eyes narrowed.

'What is it, Shannon? Can't you stand the fact that I'm seeing you as a fallible human being instead of the flawless cardboard cut-out you like to pretend to be?'

Taken aback, she could only stare at him, open-mouthed.

'Cardboard cut-out?' she echoed at last. 'I've never pretended to be any such thing.'

'Take a closer look at yourself,' he gritted. 'You're probably the only one who can. Or is your cover-up act so complete you won't even let yourself see through those damned barriers?'

She shook her head, completely mystified. 'What's this all about? Why are you attacking me all over again? I came out here to have a little fun skiing quietly round, and here you are, attempting to barge your way into my life all over again. Why can't you just leave me alone?'

His expression never wavered. 'Damned if I know.'

'Then do us both a big favour and leave me in peace,' she returned. 'I didn't ask you to come here in the first place, and I certainly didn't ask for your help out here. I can manage fine by myself.'

Dane's eyes glittered strangely, but he nodded, and swept one hand before him in a mock-courtly bow. 'Then carry on, Miss Shannon Lea. Carry on.'

Horribly aware that he was watching her every move, she tentatively slid the skis forward, uttering up a silent word of thanks when they obeyed. For a few moments she managed fairly well, taking things slowly and steadily, using the sticks to propel herself along. But, just as she was beginning to feel marginally more confident, she came to the top of a straight slope, and, before she could back off from it, found herself being carried away. The sudden movement caught her by surprise and she leaned back, attempting to slow down, only to find herself toppling over to land once more in the snow. She didn't need to look up to know he'd seen everything, and that irritated her beyond measure. Before she could get up he was skiing towards her, sliding to an expert halt at her side.

'Good lord, Shannon, what is it with you? Why are you so all-fire determined to do yourself an injury when I'm around?'

'What do you mean?' She glared back at him.

'First you try to kill yourself by running off into a blizzard, and now you risk life and limb because you can't even bring yourself to admit to me that you've never skied in your life before.' The blue eyes narrowed challengingly. 'You haven't, have you?'

Much as it infuriated her, Shannon knew when she was beaten. Refusing to meet his eyes, she shook her head. 'Never.'

He gave a single, satisfied nod. 'So why didn't you just come clean about it? Why pretend?'

'Maybe because I didn't want to give you any more reason to lord it over me.' She shot him a scathing look. 'No doubt you'd have revelled in the opportunity to play Mr Wonderful on the slopes if the roads hadn't been blocked, but frankly I didn't see any reason for giving you the chance to do the same here. And I still don't.'

'Get up.'

She bristled at the command. 'I beg your pardon?'

'You heard me. Get up. Now.'

'May I enquire why?' Her voice dripped sarcasm.

'Because if you don't I may be severely tempted to put you over my knee and give you the thrashing you sorely deserve.'

Sparks of anger danced like flames in her sherry-coloured eyes. 'That's the second time you've threatened me with violence, Mr Jacobsen,' she said evenly. 'Other women may have enjoyed your Viking tactics but, let me assure you, if you lay one finger on me you'll regret it.'

'And who's to know what I do to you out here in the middle of nowhere?' His calmness fuelled her fury still more. 'Do as you're told—or you'll be the one with regrets.'

She was tempted to call his bluff, hardly able to believe he'd carry out his threat. Then she saw the look of steely determination in his eyes and knew he was more than capable of it. Much as it pained her to meekly obey, Shannon clambered slowly to her fect, muttering darkly beneath her breath.

'Now what, Mr Jacobsen?' She gave him a saccharin-sweet smile, totally at odds with the blatant hostility in her eyes. 'Please honour me with your next command, that I may instantly leap to do your bidding.'

His mouth curved in a faint smile. 'That's better. Now, Miss Lea, I am going to teach you to ski.'

'And if I don't want to learn?'

'Then you can carry on in your bid to break as many bones as humanly possible in the shortest space of time.' He fixed her with a warning look. 'But I would ask you to remember that the roads are still blocked, and the nearest hospital is miles away. Now—do you still want to go it alone?'

Moodily she looked down at the ground. He was right. At this rate she would have an accident, and she'd only have her own stubbornness to blame for it.

'Oh, all right,' she capitulated.

'Good. Then we'll begin with some limbering-up excercises, to loosen you up and get you accustomed to the skis. Ready?'

'As I'll ever be.'

He put her through a variety of exercises, his demonstration making each one appear easier than the last. But when Shannon tried them she was dismayed to find her usual easy grace had deserted her, leaving her clumsy and uncoordinated, like a new-born foal still trying to come to terms with its own legs. She fell over several times, but came to no harm in the soft, forgiving snow. He was, to her amazement, remarkably patient with her efforts, and she found she was actually enjoying the lesson, relishing the challenge of making her body work with the skis instead of against them. But since she'd considered herself relatively fit, she was disconcerted when her muscles began aching after just a short time. When she said as much to Dane, he nodded.

'You're using muscles that don't usually get much work,' he said. 'It's quite normal to tire quickly on the slopes.'

'You don't seem to be having any problems,' she pointed out, a little grouchily.

'And nor will you when you get used to it, so stop complaining.'

'I'm not. . .'

He sighed heavily. 'Do you want to go on with the lesson, or stand about talking all day long?'

Nettled, she glared back at him. They'd managed to get through two whole sentences there without snapping each other's heads off—she should have known it could never last.

'I'm awaiting your next command,' she said evenly.

'Then we'll go for a walk.'

'A walk?' She shot him a pained look. 'But I've got six-foot-long planks of wood attached to my feet. How am I supposed to walk?'

'By making your legs do the work instead of your poor over-used mouth,' he returned drily, then set off across the field before she could reply. Shannon fell in behind him, muttering under her breath until the sheer exertion robbed her of the power of speech and she was forced to concentrate all her energy on the task in hand.

'Doing all right back there?' He glanced back over

his shoulder, and she nodded, red-faced. 'Just tell me if you need a rest.'

Right then Shannon would gladly have given her entire make-up kit for a rest, but there was no way she was about to admit any weakness to him, particularly after that crack about her 'poor over-used mouth'. So he thought she talked too much, did he? He'd see how quiet she could be—in fact, the big ox might just think he was teaching a statue, male-chauvinist pig that he was. He was clearly of the old school, which held that women belonged barefoot, pregnant—and silent—in the kitchen. Come to think of it, his Viking ancestors hadn't exactly been famed for their chivalrous treatment of women, and the traits had obviously come undiluted down the line to him.

With her head down, concentrating on pushing the skis along and her mind happily listing the insults she'd love to heap on his golden head, Shannon failed to notice that he'd come to a halt just a couple of feet in front of her, till she cannoned straight into his solid bulk, her skis sliding neatly between his. She gave a little shriek of surprise, then felt herself tipping over and grabbed at his jacket to save herself. He'd been turning round to speak to her, and the sudden movement caught him off balance, so that they tumbled unceremoniously to the ground together.

'Are you all right?'

The fall hadn't affected her in the slightest, but the shock of finding herself lying beneath Dane stunned her into silence. His face was mere inches from her own; she could feel his warm breath on her skin, and she gazed up wide-eyed, momentarily robbed of the power of speech by a strange and potent mixture of sensations invading her body.

'Shannon?'

He was so close she could feel her own name as much as hear it, and she closed her eyes, gripped by a longing more powerful than anything she'd ever known before. From a distance she heard him groan, and something deep within her revelled at the sound, her lips parting of their own accord in hunger for his kiss. It was only when his mouth claimed hers that some kind of reality surged back into her consciousness and her eyes flew wide open in horror as she belatedly realised just what was happening.

'What do you think you're doing?' She wrenched her face away from his, her breathing fast and shallow as she stared up at him, her pupils still dilated from the passion he'd stirred in her.

His answering expression was unreadable, but his voice when he answered was laden with contempt. 'I'm doing just what you wanted me to do, Shannon Lea.'

'I most certainly did not!' For once in her life she was grateful for the surge of anger welling up inside her, glad to use it as a defence, even though in her heart she knew it was directed not at Dane but at herself. 'As usual, you're simply doing what you want, with no thought of anything—or anyone—else.'

He gazed down at her for a long moment, then shook his head in disbelief.

'Sweet heaven,' he muttered. 'You're incredible, do you know that? You were begging to be kissed—frankly, it's the only honest emotion I've ever witnessed in you.'

'How dare you?' she hissed, still horribly aware of the way his body was pressing into hers. 'I want nothing from you.'

'Are you really so sure of that?' His eyes narrowed dangerously. 'I think you want everything from me, Shannon; you just haven't got the guts to admit it. I think you were shocked just now to discover the remnants of a warm human being still surviving within that ice palace you've constructed around you.'

Shaken by the image, she shook her head. 'You're wrong.'

'Am I?' He raised one eyebrow sardonically. 'Then I'll prove it to you.'

Before she even had time to realise his intentions, he drove his long, powerful fingers into her hair, bringing her face round to his, and her squeal of outrage was silenced as he took possession of her mouth. There was no gentleness in the caress this time, no tenderness in the way he raked his lips over hers, no subtlety intended when he thrust his tongue deep into her mouth, ignoring the muted whimpers of protest that died in her throat. Shannon fought against him as hard as she could, but his hands in her hair held her face captive just where he wanted it, and she was pinned to the ground by his weight. But the greatest struggle of all was against herself, she acknowledged painfully, agonisingly aware of her body's own powerful longing to press closer and closer still.

At last he raised his head, gazing down into her unfocused eyes, contemptuous triumph written all over his harsh features.

'I could take you any time I wanted, Shannon,' he said in a soft voice that sent a shiver down her spine.

'Only if you raped me,' she spat back. 'Is that how you keep your track record, Dane? By taking what you want regardless of how the other person feels?'

He shook his head. 'There would be no rape involved,' he stated quietly. 'Because underneath all that starch there's a great deal of passion in you. But I'm the only one capable of setting it alight.'

'You're what?' Even though she knew she was playing with fire, knew exactly how vulnerable she was, Shannon wanted to laugh in his arrogant face. Instead she shook her head abruptly, injecting as much scorn into her voice as she was capable of. 'I'd thank you to let me up, Mr Jacobsen. I don't wish to lie here listening to the ramblings of a madman any longer.'

For a long moment he lay where he was, and she knew a second's real apprehension. Had she pushed him too far this time? But at last he rolled over, and she clambered slowly to her feet, forcing herself to meet his eyes.

'Now,' she said steadily, 'I suggest for both our sakes we forget what happened here just now. We're stuck in this place for the time being, and it appears there's nothing we can do about that. But I suggest we attempt to stay out of each other's way as much as possible, under the circumstances. I'm going back to the cottage now. You can do what you like.' Turning away, she bent to pick up her skis and sticks, then began walking away from him, only releasing a pent-up breath when it became clear he wasn't going to follow her.

Back in the cottage she took a long, hot bath, but the water failed to ease the tension in her body, even though she lay there for what seemed like an eternity, trying to will away the effects of the afternoon. Dane had stirred something up within her, disturbed deep pools that had perhaps never been touched before, and she hadn't thc faintest idea how to go about calming those waters again. The worst part lay in facing up to the fact that some of the things he'd said were true, much as she might try to deny it. No other man had ever managed even to light a spark within her, yet *he* had set her body aflame, and it had taken every ounce of will-power she possessed not to give in to the longing he'd unleashed.

'Oh, Mama, is this how it was for you?' she murmured aloud to the empty room. 'Did you go a little bit crazy when my father kissed you?' It was ironic to realise she'd once come close to despising her mother for that frailty, when she was battling hard now not to fall into the same trap herself. But battle she must if she was to survive this ridiculous situation. Other women might be able to cope with an affair that was based on passion and nothing else, but she knew herself well enough to realise she could only be permanently scarred by such an involvement.

Out there in the cold snow Dane Jacobsen had stripped away some of the barriers she protected herself with. But she could rebuild them. She had to.

CHAPTER FOUR

THAT evening Shannon steered well clear of Dane, all but tiptoeing around him, determined not to land in any more confrontations. From now till this snow siege ended, she would simply live under the same roof, but keep to her own side of an invisible barrier, she decided. She could only hope he'd do the same. A few times she was aware that he was watching her, but managed every time to resist the temptation to look up, unsure of just what she might see in his eyes. It was barely eight o'clock when she decided she might as well go to bed, but, when she headed towards the kitchen to make a suppertime hot drink, he followed her.

'What are you doing, Shae?'

'I thought I'd turn in for the night.'

'It's early.'

She nodded. 'I know. But all this fresh air has made me tired.' She looked up at him with a falsely bright smile, then wished she hadn't. Dressed in a plaid shirt and faded jeans that clung lovingly to his muscular thighs, he was leaning against the door-jamb with his usual easy animal grace, and she was forced to swallow hard against a rush of desire that totally unnerved her. What was happening to her? she wondered hazily; after this afternoon she should surely loathe the man more than ever. Instead, here she was, going weak at the knees like an adolescent schoolgirl. Suddenly a thought struck her and her eyes grew puzzled. 'What did you call me just now?'

'Shae.' The blue eyes regarded her steadily. 'Do you object to your name being shortened?'

She shook her head. 'No. But only my friends call me Shae.'

'And I don't qualify?'

She turned away from his probing eyes, busying herself by filling the kettle at the sink. 'I barely know you.'

He gave a little grunt of exasperation. 'How well do you have to know someone before you call them friend?'

She lifted her narrow shoulders. 'It's not something that can be measured in time. Many other things come into it.'

'Such as?'

'Such as—understanding. Compassion. Trust.'

'Ah, yes—trust.' He seemed to examine the word, turning it over like a rare gem. 'Aye, there's the rub. Something tells me that's the keyword in your life.'

'Isn't it in everyone's?' She bridled at the coolly assessing tone of his voice.

'Perhaps.' He rubbed his chin thoughtfully. 'But many people prefer to start off on a basis of trust, rather than insist it be won.'

'Then they're fools.' The vehemence of her answer surprised both of them. 'They're asking for trouble—disillusionment at the very least, more probably betrayal.' To her horror she felt the sting of tears in her eyes and looked away again, refusing to let him see her moment of weakness.

'What has happened in your life to make you so

afraid, Shannon?' The quietly spoken words fell on her like stinging blows.

'Not afraid,' she retorted sharply. 'Cynical.'

'Scratch a cynic and you'll generally find a frightened soul beneath the hard shell.'

'Look.' She squared up to him, tilting her chin resolutely. 'You want to call me Shae? Fine—frankly I couldn't care less if you call me Rin-Tin-Tin, only let's not get into a profound discussion about the psychological implications of it all.'

His lips quirked at the corners. '"What's in a name?", indeed? Perhaps even more than the Bard himself realised.' He paused for a moment, eyeing her consideringly. 'Do you trust me?'

Forgetting her own resolve not to get into any more confrontations, Shannon gave a hollow laugh. 'You can really ask that after what happened today?'

'What did happen today?'

'What did happen?' She threw the words back at him incredulously. 'Why, weren't you there, Dane? I'll tell you what happened today—a man I barely know forced himself on me in a snowy field, that's what happened today.'

To her fury her impassioned words seemed to amuse him.

'Forced himself on you?' he echoed. 'And tell me, my sweet, coy little virgin, what did you do to deserve such a terrible fate?'

'I did nothing,' she said through gritted teeth. 'Nothing at all.'

'Oh, but I think you did,' he returned evenly. 'I think you asked for everything you got, and a whole lot besides. Furthermore, I think you enjoyed every second of it, until something in your tight little Calvinistic soul reared up in protest.'

'Is that the best explanation you can come up with for the fact that I don't lie down and beg you to take me?' she shot back, her temper well and truly up now. 'Hasn't it ever occurred to you that I find you repulsive—that I'd rather be kissed by a lizard than you?'

'How well you lie to yourself,' he said. 'But your body didn't lie to me this afternoon. For just a few minutes out there I was holding a real live flesh-and-blood woman in my arms.'

Abruptly she looked away from him, painfully aware that he was speaking only the truth.

'You took me by surprise,' she muttered.

'I didn't take you at all,' he returned swiftly. 'I accepted what you offered—freely.'

'Then I hope you made the most of it, Mr Jacobsen.' Her eyes glittered strangely as she gazed up at him. 'Because it will never be offered again.' She took a deep breath, desperately trying to calm the turmoil raging within. 'Now, if you'll excuse me, I'm going to bed.'

He was still barring the doorway, and for a second she thought he'd refuse to move. But he took a step back, sweeping his arm into a mocking bow.

'Sweet dreams in your cold virgin bed, Miss Lea. Sweet dreams.'

It was only when she reached the bedroom that Shannon realised she'd forgotten to take her coffee with her. Well, not for a king's ransom would she return to the kitchen, even though she really could do with the drink. It didn't even matter that coffee would probably keep her awake—in her present state of mind she'd never be able to sleep anyway.

She sat down before the dressing-table, automatically picking up a hairbrush, but the sight of her own reflection in the mirror distracted her, and for long moments she simply stared at her own face, as if seeing it through the eyes of a stranger. What was it about her that apparently attracted him? She was no beauty, though she was realistic enough to accept there must be something appealing in the small, heart-shaped face with its delicate, finely boned features. Her large, sherry-coloured eyes, always her best feature, held shadows tonight, and she wondered about that. Shadows of past ghosts still—or of much more recent sorrows?

She shook her head, tugging the hairbrush vigorously through her tangled auburn locks. Nothing that had happened recently had caused her pain, she told herself adamantly—anger certainly, and annoyance in abundance, but not pain. So why was there an ache in her heart? Because, if she was honest with herself, she was rejecting something she wanted badly, but couldn't allow herself to have. Oh, she could fall into Dane's arms easily enough; she'd discovered to her cost just how easily out in the snow today. Then she'd become just another notch on his bedpost—another victory, albeit not won with quite his usual ease. She couldn't bear that—couldn't stand to become just another in a long line of faceless women whose names he probably couldn't even remember. All she could do was keep him at arm's length—and pray for the strength to keep on doing it till they were released from their snowy prison.

* * *

'The roads are clear.'

Shannon turned from thc window, blinking in surprise at the unexpected sound of his voice. She must have been a hundred miles away, she realised, trying to get her thoughts together.

'I beg your pardon?'

'You heard me. The roads are clear.'

'How do you know?'

His eyes creased impatiently. 'Radio report earlier. And I took a walk along our side-road just to check. The ploughs have done a good job.'

'Oh.' She looked down at the floor, wondering why the news didn't make her feel more elated. She could leave now, could get away from Dane and the cottage, back to her own life and reality. There was no earthly reason to stay. 'I'll start packing, then.'

'Packing?'

She nodded.

'But the cottage is rented till tomorrow.'

'I know.'

'Then why leave now?'

She glanced up at him, faintly puzzled by the question. Surely he should be glad to see her go?

'After coming all this way up here you're going to leave without trying out your new skills on the proper slopes?'

She managed a faint smile. 'I don't think my skills are terribly extensive,' she demurred. 'Perhaps another time.'

'In other words you're running away,' he said flatly.

A tiny spark flared in her eyes. 'Running away from what?'

He shrugged. 'From me.'

'Don't be ridiculous. Why should I do that?'

He took a step towards her, and it was all she could do not to back away.

'Because you're afraid.'

'Of you?' She tried to laugh, but it was a shaky effort. 'That's the craziest thing I've ever heard.'

He nodded. 'Then you're afraid of yourself—afraid you won't be able to keep up the fight against the part of you that dares to be human.'

'That's not true.'

'Isn't it?' Dane raised one eyebrow consideringly. 'Then prove it. Stay another day. Come to the slopes with me.' His lips quirked in amusement. 'We'll be surrounded by dozens of people—you'll be well protected.'

'Oh, all right.' She was suddenly too weary to argue. And who knew—perhaps surrounded by people they would manage to make it through one whole day without fighting? That at least would give her one pleasant memory to take away from this whole crazy weekend.

'Go and get changed. I'll meet you back here in twenty minutes.'

As he'd predicted, the slopes were indeed busy, and she watched in envious amazement as the experienced skiers zig-zagged their way down fearsome-looking runs, as brightly clad as butterflies and apparently just as agile.

'Good heavens!' she breathed, watching one figure speeding over the snow at a break-neck pace, yet seemingly in effortless control. 'He's incredible.'

Dane nodded. 'He's pretty good.'

'Pretty good?' She eyed him wonderingly. 'Is that all you can say?'

'I've seen better.'

'Including yourself, I suppose?'

His eyes narrowed, and she felt a flicker of annoyance, this time aimed at herself. Why on earth did she always feel this need to antagonise him? she wondered irritably. Why couldn't she let the sleeping lion lie? Perhaps it was because she'd already seen countless admiring female eyes slide in his direction; even though they apparently hadn't recognised him in his goggles and ski-hat, still they were drawn by the sheer animal magnetism of the man. He couldn't disguise that.

'Still determined to play the shrew, I see,' he said coldly.

She winced at the faint trace of disgust in his voice, but managed to turn it into a careless shrug.

'Not at all. I was merely asking a question. Are you a better skier?'

He nodded. 'Yes.'

'Then please don't let me keep you down here on the baby-slopes. I'm quite sure you'd rather be up there strutting your stuff with the other ski gods.'

His blue eyes held shards of ice as he glared down at her, his features darkening in annoyance. 'Why is it that every time you open that pretty little mouth of yours a viper speaks?' he said angrily. 'Are you incapable of plain, old-fashioned pleasantness?' Without waiting for an answer he ploughed straight on. 'I *will* go on to the senior slopes, but not because I have anything to prove—to you or anyone else. Frankly it'll be a pleasure just to get the hell away from you for a while.'

As he turned away from her to head towards one of the tow-lifts, Shannon smiled a little sadly, not really sure whether she'd won or lost that particular skirmish. When she'd thrown the challenge at him a part of her had wanted him to refuse to go, had wanted him to say he'd rather stay with her. But why on earth had she been so prickly if she'd wanted him to stay? Because her only defence was to turn him against her, she realised with a pang of sorrow. She couldn't ever show him 'plain, old-fashioned pleasantness' because, with him, she was constantly on a knife-edge, terrified that one false move would end in a catastrophic tumble.

She stayed where she was, waiting to see him come down the senior run, and her first sight of his black-suited figure made the breath catch in her throat. He was right; he was better than the other skier she'd been so impressed by. Moving over the snow, he was like a bird in flight, twisting and turning with total ease, at one with the elements. Tears came into her eyes as she watched him, though she couldn't have said why, but she did know it was something she'd never forget, etched on her memory now forever.

'Just look at that guy go!'

She'd been so caught up in her thoughts that the voice near her side came as a shock, but even as she turned she realised the words hadn't been aimed at her. The speaker was a tall, long-legged blonde, her wide-set brown eyes focused solely on Dane as he sped down the slope. At her side stood two other women, their admiring expressions mirror-images of the blonde's.

'He is something else on skis,' the darker of the two murmured appreciatively.

'He's something else full stop,' the blonde said. 'When did you last see a honey like him?'

'Probably the last time I went to the cinema,' the last member of the trio, a small, mousy-haired woman, chimed in, a littly archly. 'Don't tell me you two haven't realised who he is?'

On cue they turned to her, their eyes wide in anticipation.

'Well, don't make us beg for it, Suzie,' thc blonde said impatiently. 'Who is it?'

Suzie smiled, a secretive little catlike smile. 'I saw him at the tow-lift earlier,' she rev ealed. 'He'd taken his goggles off. I'd know those blue eyes anywhere.'

'For the love of Pete!' Her dark-haired friend all but screamed at her. 'Who is it?'

Suzie looked from one to the other, obviously enjoying her moment of glory. 'Dane Jacobsen,' she said slowly, clearly relishing the looks on her companions' faces.

'You're kidding me!' The blonde looked suitably awestruck. 'I've been crazy about him ever since the first time I saw him.'

Suzie gave a derisive little snort. 'You and a few thousand other women. Show me a woman who says Dane Jacobsen doesn't make her go weak at the knees and I'll show you a liar!'

'Come on,' the blonde said decisively. 'He's about to go and join the tow queue again. Let's join him.'

'Do you think we should?' Suzie frowned uncertainly. 'Don't you think he deserves a break? Perhaps he wants to be left alone.'

'Don't be daft. He's a man, isn't he? Anyway, I bet he's just as fond of the ladies as they are of him.'

They skied off together, chattering and giggling like a trio of schoolgirls, as Shannon reluctantly watched. She wanted to turn away, but some masochistic streak kept her eyes glued to the scene. He'd be nice to them, she knew. He had a reputation for being unfailingly gracious to fans, no matter how gushing they were. And who was she trying to kid, anyway? she thought unhappily. After the last couple of days spent in her company, he'd probably be more than delighted to welcome Suzie and her two glamorous friends.

As she watched, they skied straight up to him, and he turned, a faintly quizzical expression on his face which turned almost immediately to a smile. Even though she'd expected it, that smile twisted in Shannon's heart like a dagger. He'd never smiled at her like that.

She turned away, feeling sick at heart, even though she knew she should be glad. She'd lost him now—he'd probably forget she was even there, and who could blame him? Well, it was all to the good; after he'd finished skiing for the day they'd return to the cottage, and she'd set out for home. The prospect of spending another night under the same roof was just too much to cope with. And then it would all be over—this crazy situation which should never have happened in the first place.

She was in the cafeteria a short while later, steadfastly keeping her back to the huge windows with their wonderful view of the skiers outside, when a hand descended on to her shoulder, making her start in alarm.

'We're going home now.'

Perplexed, she looked up into Dane's face. 'Home? But you've only been skiing for a short while. Surely you're not tired of it already?'

He gave a wintry little smile. 'Not tired of the skiing, no. Let's just say the company is getting a little too exuberant for my tastes.'

She knew it was ridiculous, but his words gave her a strange little tingle deep inside, and she was forced to smother the smile that kept trying to push its way to her lips. Instead she nodded solemnly. 'Don't tell me you'd rather be in *my* company?'

He slanted a warning look at her. 'Don't push your luck, Shannon.'

'What if I say I want to stay a while longer?' she asked teasingly.

'If you'd like to find out what it's like to be put over my knee and given a good thrashing in a public place that's probably the best way to do it.'

Her good humour abruptly vanished. So much for that fleeting little moment of innocent fun.

'What's the matter, Dane?' she said coldly. 'Is the strain of being a big star finally beginning to get to you?'

'Lady, the so-called strain of being a big star is nothing compared to the strain of just being with you,' he shot back.

She winced, surprised to find how much she was hurt by the stinging acid in his voice, even though she knew she'd brought it on herself.

'Now,' he said through gritted teeth, 'would you care to make a big scene in front of all the other diners, or would you like to walk out of here under your own steam?'

She made no answer, but rose from the chair, knowing when she was beaten, even though she was fuming inside at his high-handedness. In a choice between meekly obeying his commands and being publicly humiliated there really was no choice. Dane might be an arrogant, pig-headed ox, but he was also more than capable of carrying out his threats.

She raged silently all the way back to the cottage, but it was only when the front door closed behind them that she could trust herself enough to speak.

'Just what was all that about?'

He raised one eyebrow questioningly. 'All what, exactly?'

'The lord-and-master routine back there in the cafeteria. You ordered me to leave!'

'And you, acting sensibly for once in your life, obeyed the order.'

'What gives you the right to tell me what to do?' Despite her resolution to stay calm, Shannon could feel her temper rising, bringing an unwanted heat to her pale skin.

'Somebody needs to.' His voice was even, yet she could hear his displeasure, loud and clear.

'And you think you're the one?' she shot the words back scathingly. 'Just because you could have twisted those three bimbos round your little finger this afternoon, don't assume all women are cut from the same cloth.' Unbidden, Suzie's words came back to her. 'Show me a woman who says Dane Jacobsen doesn't make her go weak at the knees, and I'll show you a liar!' At one time she'd have sworn with hand on heart that Dane had absolutely no effect on her knees whatsoever. But now?

She looked away from him, all too horribly aware of the truth. Even when he was coldly angry, as now, something inside her longed to simply reach out to him. Earlier today she'd been jealous because he'd smiled at the three women in a way he'd never smiled at her. But if he did—oh, sweet heaven, if he did, if he showed just one moment of softness, she'd be lost. Maybe that was why she'd been so uncharacteristically antagonistic to him all along, she realised now. But it was getting harder with every moment she spent with him.

'I'm going home this evening,' she announced, forcing herself to speak calmly. 'Frankly I don't see any point in staying till morning and subjecting myself to yet another evening of arguments.' She looked at him expectantly, but rather to her surprise he merely nodded for her to continue. 'I'm going to go and take a bath, then I'll pack. We may as well say goodbye now.'

His eyebrows quirked wryly. 'I think our paths will cross again, Shannon Lea,' he said evenly.

'For the sake of the few unfrazzled nerve-endings I have left, I sincerely hope not, Mr Jacobsen,' she returned coolly, completely unaware that she'd crossed her fingers behind her back in the old childhood gesture of protection against telling a lie. Then she turned towards the stairs, resisting with all her strength the temptation to turn back for one last glance of the man who'd sent her normally sane and steady world into turmoil.

She lay for a long time in the enveloping warmth of the bath-water, feeling a strange sense of sadness. It was all over—she could go home now, could continue with the rest of her life as though this ridiculous weekend had never happened. She slid deeper into the water with a sigh. Who was she trying to kid? She'd only been in Dane's company for a matter of days, but he'd left a mark on her, a mark it could prove impossible to erase.

At last she rose from the water, wrapping a towel about her damp body as she walked to her room, mentally weighed down by her thoughts, and physically wearied, too. Right now she couldn't even face the thought of the long drive home—but a short rest would set her back on her feet again. She lay down on the bed intending simply to relax and restore herself, but within minutes she was deeply asleep, her red-gold hair fanning out like tongues of fire over the white pillows.

She never knew how long she slept, but when she drifted back to consciousness she was aware even before opening her eyes that she was no longer alone in the room, and her body stiffened.

'It's all right.' Dane's voice came softly to her through the darkness. 'I came to see if you were OK. You've been asleep for a long time.'

Shannon felt the bed sink slightly as he sat down beside her, and suddenly realised to her horror that the towel she'd wrapped about herself had slipped off as she slept. But, before she could find it in the darkness, he switched on the bedside lamp, and her face flamed with colour as he turned to look at her, his eyes darkening as they swept freely over her nakedness. Instinctively she made to cover her breasts, but he caught her arm.

'Don't,' he said quietly. 'Don't hide from me.'

She closed her eyes, desperately trying to find the anger which had protected her from him so far, but found only an overwhelming longing to simply lose herself in his arms.

'Dane.' His name on her lips was like a plea, and with one swift movement he gathered her into his arms, pressing her against his powerful chest.

'You're beautiful,' he murmured huskily, burying his hands in her cascade of hair to bring her closer still.

She tried to pull away, but as she moved her head it brought her closer to his mouth, and when his lips touched hers she was lost, caught up in an explosion triggered by his touch. Her hands slid up his arms to grip his shoulders, her fingers digging into the soft material of his shirt as though he alone could anchor her. She was dizzy, intoxicated, unable to think straight as he pushed her back against the pillows, his body covering hers, her senses swimming with the urgent pressure of him between her naked thighs.

She hardly knew what she was doing, barely realised that she was starting to unbutton his shirt, her fingers trembling in their haste to feel his skin, and he laughed deep in his throat, a glorying, exultantly male sound that thrilled the woman in her. Impatiently he finished the task, ripping the material from his shoulders and tossing it to the floor. The breath caught in her throat at the sight of his broad chest with its thick mat of glistening golden hair. He pulled away long enough to strip off the rest of his clothes, and she followed, unable to bear losing contact even for a second, dipping her head forwards to taste his skin, her fingers stroking his muscled back.

He turned to her, gathering her in his arms, and they rolled in glorious abandon on the roomy expanse of bed, a wanton tangle of limbs. They were like two starving people falling on an unexpected feast, tasting freely of one another. She drank in the clean masculine smell of him, revelling in the power of the arms that held her so tightly, the tenderness of the hands that caressed her heated skin. His mouth explored her eager breasts and she arched up towards him, her responses instinctive, untutored, yet driving him wild with her undisguised need.

'Shannon.' His voice was raggedly urgent, and she gazed up at him through cloudy, unfocused eyes. He smiled, touching her cheek as though in apology. 'Sweetheart, are you protected?'

The words were tenderly spoken, yet they hit her like a tidal wave of icy-cold water, instantly extinguishing the flames of passion curling inside her, bringing her to horrified realisation of just what she was doing. She stared wordlessly at him for a moment, her eyes wide with dismay. How could she, of all people, have come so perilously close to being swept away by desire?

'It's all right,' he said, clearly misinterpreting her reaction. 'I can take care of things.'

'No!' Her hand shot out to grasp his arm as he made to move away.

He reached out to stroke her hair, frowning as she froze beneath his touch. 'What is it, Shannon? Are you still a virgin? Don't worry, I would never hurt you.'

Her eyes were dark and haunted in her pale face. 'You don't understand.'

'Then talk to me, Shannon,' he urged. 'Tell me why.'

She shook her head, sending her hair tumbling wildly about her bare shoulders. 'I can't.'

'Talk to me.'

'I can't!'

'Shannon.' He gripped her none too gently by the shoulders. 'Look at me.'

Driven into a corner, she panicked, her arms flailing

desperately as she tried to wrench herself free, but he held on tight.

'Why can't you just leave me alone?' Her voice held the anguish of years, and his eyes darkened as he gazed down into her tortured face.

'Good grief, Shannon,' he murmured. 'What's happened in your life to make you like this?'

She was pierced by his compassion, powerless to stem the flood of tears welling up as though a dam had finally burst within her. Racked by sobs, she tried again to pull away, but he gathered her into his arms, holding her shaking body against his own, his fingers stroking her hair.

When the storm finally passed, she was spent, exhausted, and she lay against him, too worn out to fight any longer. He was silent, but she could sense anger burning slowly inside him and wondered if it was directed at her. Was he furious because she'd led him on only to change her mind at the last minute? To be honest, she couldn't really blame him if he did feel that way, though none of her own actions had been deliberate.

She gazed unseeingly across the room, ashamed of her own weakness, all too aware of her vulnerability. Her defences had crumbled under the onslaught of tears; now she lay in his arms, naked emotionally as much as physically. When the questions began, as they surely must, there was nothing left within her to protect her from his probing.

'Shannon?' His voice came softly to her, and she tensed, awaiting the inevitable interrogation.

'Yes?' she murmured dully.

'Rest now. Just let go. Nothing can harm you here.'

Gratitude washed over her in a warm wave, sending

fresh tears to her eyes, and she buried her face in his shoulder, moved beyond words by his understanding. A deep sigh shuddered through her body as she relaxed against him, realising with a profound sense of wonder that, for the first time in her life, she felt secure.

She woke some time in the night, disoriented, wondering where on earth she was. Then she heard the sounds of rhythmic breathing and realised Dane was sleeping at her side. As memory returned she was hit by a depression close to despair, the earlier feeling of security completely vanished. She should never have let go—should never have cried so desperately in his arms. Now he knew that something in her life had caused her great pain and, even though he couldn't possibly have any idea what it had been, still she was racked by his knowing even that much about her.

Worse still was the realisation of how close she'd come to making love with him. History had tried to repeat itself, she realised bitterly; she'd allowed a man to sweep her off her feet with honeyed words—just as her mother had before her. She'd always considered herself so strong, so immune to the temptations of the flesh; yet last night she'd discovered a depth of passion within her that had shaken her profoundly. But it hadn't simply been desire, she acknowledged painfully—desire she could have handled. She'd found something else in Dane's strong arms; he'd unleashed a longing, a need, not just for physical satisfaction, but for something far, far greater.

Shannon lay back against the pillows, squeezing her eyes tight shut, as though that could block out the awful truth. The longing he'd kindled within her had been for love—his love. Suddenly she knew she couldn't face him again in this new vulnerability—couldn't look into his eyes and see sympathy. He might be kind, gentle even, but his words would be no more than a courteous cloak of indifference; for hadn't she now joined the ranks of women who wanted him? She hadn't made love with him, but for him the battle had already been won, and she would no longer present a challenge. She couldn't face seeing that realisation in his eyes, for the sake of her own sanity had to get away—had to flee from him for a second time. Only this time she had to succeed.

Moving with agonising stealth, she slipped from beneath the covers and began dressing, grateful that the jogging-suit she'd left draped over the chair had no noisy zips to be contended with. Dane muttered something, and she froze, but after a moment he rolled over, and the sounds of his breathing told her he'd fallen into a still deeper sleep. There was no time to pack, and she'd make too much noise rummaging for clothes. She'd just have to send for the rest of her things.

At the door Shannon turned back, unable to leave without seeing his face one last time. Moonlight shone into the room, its rays casting shadows over his hawklike profile, and tears blurred her eyes at the sight. He was in her heart now, she realised bleakly, seared into her soul like a brand.

'Goodbye, my love,' she whispered into the silence. 'I'll never forget you.'

She crept downstairs, remembering to avoid the creaking step, and padded softly across the living-room floor, hardly daring to breathe as she opened the front door. Inside, a dull, leaden weight settled deep within her, crushing all the foolish, foolish hopes she'd allowed to grow almost without realising it. Well, they were better dead. To allow them to flourish could lead only to pain—even greater pain than she was feeling in this moment, though she could hardly imagine anything could be greater.

Reaching her car at last, she drove away into the silent night, gazing through a gauze of tears over the snow-covered mountains ahead.

The flat seemed cold and empty when she let herself in several hours later, and discovering a message from Kelly on the answering-machine brought no respite from the depression which had settled over her like a heavy black cloud. She spun the tape on and a polite Scottish voice informed her that her services were required by an independent television company about to start work on a drama based on the oil business, to be set largely around Aberdeen. If she was interested, the voice said, could she please get in touch as soon as possible?

She played the message over again, grabbing a note-pad from the desk to jot down the number. Given the choice, she'd really rather have had an assignment in Outer Mongolia or possibly Timbuktu—maybe by putting a few thousand miles between herself and Dane she'd manage to get him out of her mind.

A faint, ironic smile touched her lips. Who was she trying to kid? Even if she jumped on the next space shuttle to Mars it wouldn't make any difference. Dane Jacobsen was lodged firmly and irrevocably in her heart. No distance could alter that.

CHAPTER FIVE

SHANNON woke with tears still damp on her face. It was that dream again—the one which had haunted her sleep almost every night for the past three weeks. A dream in which she stood in a glorious, sweet-scented, flower-filled garden watching a tall, golden-haired man playing with beautiful blonde, blue-eyed children, all miniature replicas of himself. In the dream she was smiling, holding out her hands to the man and the children, but her smile slowly faded as she realised they couldn't see her. She opened her mouth to call out to them, but no sound emerged. She tried to walk over the rich green grass towards them, but her feet seemed glued in place. Even as she watched, the idyllic little world began to fade, leaving her alone and in tears for a world so cruelly offered, then snatched away.

It didn't take a Freud to work out the significance of that dream, she thought dully, making her way to the tiny cabinet which the hotel proprietors chose to call a private bathroom. It was a subconscious form of mourning for a foolish love she'd allowed to spring to life in her heart, only to kill stone dead—except that her feelings for Dane were far from dead, she acknowledged ruefully. Even now, three weeks after she'd driven away from that little cottage near Glenshee, he was still imprinted on her heart like a brand.

Ordinarily she'd have enjoyed the assignment—the cast and crew were a nice bunch for the most part, and she'd always liked Aberdeen. But it seemed nothing could drag her thoughts away from Dane for long—he was always there on the edges of her mind, hovering like a kestrel ready to pounce on unsuspecting prey.

Desperate to find some release, Shannon tried taking long, solitary walks along the city's golden shoreline, hunching her shoulders into a warm sheepskin jacket against the biting chill of the ever-present north-sea wind. When that didn't work, she dived into a frantic round of socialising, accepting every invitation to drinks and dinner passed her way by the amiable camera crew. But it seemed even that could do little more than dull the edges of the pain, and, when she woke up one morning with a painful hangover and realised the ache in her heart was just as strong as it had ever been, she swore she'd never again attempt to deal with her sorrows that way.

Today was the last day of the assignment. Normally that would have made her feel a little melancholy, for she'd never grown accustomed to the frequent farewells that were an inevitable part of her professional life. Instead she simply felt that same old dull ache like a weight about her heart, dragging her down, making everything else seem pointless.

She gazed dispiritedly at her own reflection in the mirror, seeing the dark shadows beneath her eyes. She'd lost weight over the past three weeks; now her features seemed positively angular, and her skin was as pale as to be almost translucent. If Kelly could see her now she'd throw up her hands in horror and drag her off to the nearest restaurant to order the biggest meal on the menu.

The thought made her smile wryly. By rights she

should blame Kelly for all of this. If she hadn't reneged on her promise to go to Glenshee, Dane would never have followed her to that tiny cottage. Yet, for all the sadness she was suffering now, Shannon couldn't find it within herself to wish it had all never happened. Being with Dane had changed her—eventually she'd be the richer for that, even if right now all she could feel was anguish.

She dressed listlessly, not bothering with make-up. Cosmetics might conceal the pallor of her skin, but it could never hide the shadows in her eyes. She took one last glance in the mirror before leaving the room, sighing dispiritedly at the sight of her own reflection. She'd never been a raving beauty, it was true, but at the moment she looked a wreck. Dane Jacobsen had a lot to answer for.

Despite all, she enjoyed the last day on set. The cast and crew were in a high-spirited, end-of-term frame of mind, and the mood was catching.

'Do you know, this is the first time I've really seen you laughing?' Jack Bryson, the chief cameraman, told her as they waited for the director's 'OK' to strike the set, a quizzical grin seaming his weather-beaten face. 'Have we really been such a bunch of miseries to work with?'

'No, it's not that.' She gave him an apologetic little smile. 'I've had things on my mind, that's all.'

He nodded understandingly. 'Must have been pretty weighty things, Shannon. Want to talk about them?'

She shook her head. 'No. Don't worry, though. I can work them out for myself.'

He regarded her gravely, the amusement dying from his expression. 'It's a mistake to bottle things up, sweetheart,' he said, and the sympathy in his voice brought a lump to her throat. 'You shouldn't try to shoulder burdens all by yourself.'

She laid a hand on his arm, her eyes warm. 'I'll be fine, Jack,' she said softly, appreciating his concern. 'It's nothing serious.'

The sideways look he sent her clearly said he was far from convinced, but to her relief he let the subject drop.

'So where are you heading off to now?' he asked. 'Or are you taking a break?'

'I had thought about it,' she returned, 'but I had a fairly frantic call from a theatre director down in Sheffield.' She frowned, remembering the call. 'For some reason he was adamant that he simply had to have me for the make-up on the new play he's doing.'

'Oh?' Jack raised his bushy eyebrows questioningly. 'Have you done much theatre work?'

'Bits and pieces. Not enough to get my name known in those circles, I wouldn't have thought.' She gave a little shrug. 'Still, who am I to look gift work in the mouth, no matter where it comes from?'

Jack grinned. 'You're good at your job,' he said. 'You'll never have to worry about where the next assignment's coming from.'

'I hope you're right.'

They were interrupted then by the arrival of the director's production assistant, who'd been sent to tell everyone they could 'wrap' for the day.

'And, indeed, for the whole shoot,' Jack murmured appreciatively, getting to his feet. 'Come on, Shannon, we all deserve a celebratory drink for our efforts. The director's buying.'

The 'celebratory drink' fast developed into a full-scale party, but Shannon managed to make her excuses and leave, knowing she had a long drive ahead of her. Rehearsals on the Sheffield play didn't actually begin till two days later, but she'd promised to be there as soon as she could to discuss make-up with the director. It sounded like an interesting job—the play was a futuristic drama set in the twenty-first century, and the director said she'd have a chance to really let her imagination run riot on the styles.

'To a certain extent you'll have free rein,' he'd told her over the telephone. 'I'll just give you the overall concept of the thing, and it's up to you how to interpret as you see fit.'

Shannon took that with a pinch of salt, knowing from experience how few directors really were willing to give 'free rein' to any of the technicians on the crew. Still, it sounded like a fascinating challenge, and she'd never been to Sheffield before, so it would give her an opportunity to see another little bit of the world. If truth were told, she still didn't care much where she was, she admitted reluctantly, because the one place in the world she longed to be was at Dane's side, and that was strictly out of bounds.

The next day found her drivng round the busy, bustling city of Sheffield, desperately trying to keep one eye on the traffic, and the other on the directions scrawled on a piece of paper. The director had told her most of the cast and crew were staying in the same hotel, and a room had been reserved for her there, too. Now all she had to do was find it.

'Eureka!' she muttered triumphantly as she finally spotted the elusive hotel, and drew into its car park.

'I was beginning to think this place must be a figment of someone's imagination.'

'My name's Shannon Lea,' she told the receptionist, an attractive brunette. 'I believe a reservation has been made for me.'

The woman looked at her, an unmistakably speculative gleam in her hazel eyes, and Shannon frowned, wondering at the look.

'Ah, yes, Miss Lea. A room has indeed been booked for you. It's on the second floor, number twenty-seven.'

Shannon signed the register and took the key, still puzzled by the receptionist's knowing look. Then she shrugged. She was imagining things. Or else the poor woman couldn't help the way she looked; perhaps it had something to do with those finely arched eyebrows of hers.

She made her way to the second floor, her frown deepening as she looked about her, properly taking in her surroundings for the first time. The hotel was a good one, not luxurious, but considerably better than she was accustomed to staying in while working. She made a mental note to check the tariff later with the receptionist—there would be little point in living so comfortably for a few weeks if the bill swallowed most of her wages at the end of it.

Her room was small but nicely furnished, and she smiled at the sight of a posy of flowers in a vase on the dressing-table. Nice touch. This could turn out to be a really nice job if the director was always this considerate.

She unpacked quickly and changed from her travelling clothes into jeans and a warm sweatshirt, stopping to twist her unruly auburn curls into a topknot, then returned to Reception to ask for directions to the theatre.

'Oh, you'll find it very easily,' the woman said pleasantly. 'It's just a couple of hundred yards further down the road. Well within walking distance.'

'That's probably why most of the cast and crew are staying here, I suppose?' Shannon said.

The woman smiled, a little archly. 'Some of them are,' she returned. 'I wouldn't say most of them.'

Shannon frowned. 'But I thought. . .'

The woman's smile never wavered. 'You thought. . .?'

Shannon shook her head. 'It doesn't matter.' She turned to move away, then glanced back. 'Didn't the director simply make a block-booking here?'

The woman shook her head. 'The director didn't, no.'

'His assistant, then,' Shae returned a little impatiently, struck by a strange feeling that she was being toyed with.

It was the receptionist's turn to look faintly puzzled. 'No-one made any block-bookings at all,' she said. 'As far as I understand it, the individual actors made their own arrangements.'

Shannon gave a tiny shrug, giving up the struggle to understand. She was seeing mysteries where there were none, she told herself irritably. The director had probably taken a room for her there tonight assuming she'd look for somthing more suited to her purse in her own time.

Following the directions she'd been given, Shannon came to the theatre stage door a few minutes later. She gave her name to the elderly man on duty there, and he nodded.

'You're expected. Go on through.'

There was something about the atmosphere of a theatre that never failed to stir her blood, Shannon mused as she walked along the corridors. Even now, when the place was virtually empty, it seemed to hold echoes and shadows of all the people who'd been here, and all the characters they'd played. She found the make-up room and went in, a faint smile playing about her lips as she looked round. Bare, a little shabby, sorely in need of a fresh coat of paint, yet the room excited her in a way she could never have explained.

She spotted a sheet of paper lying on the dressing-table and wondered if it might be a message for her. But when she looked at it more closely, the blood rushed from her face and she gave a little gasp of incredulous horror. The paper was a poster advertising the play Shannon was to be working on—a poster dominated by the vivid blue eyes and harsh, hawklike features of the star player. A sound at the door caught her attention and she turned abruptly, shock still clear on her face.

'Hello, Shannon.'

'Dane?' Even though he was standing in front of her, barely a few feet away, she could still barely believe the evidence of her own eyes.

'In the flesh.'

She stared at him in silence for a moment, then shook her head as though that could clear the confusion fogging her brain. Then she frowned.

'You don't seem surprised to see me.'

He regarded her steadily. 'I'm not.'

'Did the director mention he'd taken me on?'

'No.'

'Then how. . .?'

'I told him to hire you.'

It took a moment for that to sink in. Then her eyes widened in amazement.

'You did what?'

'You heard.'

'I might have heard, but I'm not at all sure I believed what I heard,' she muttered, searching his face for clues, but finding none. 'Why, Dane?'

His eyes glittered strangely. 'Maybe because I don't like unfinished business.'

'Any business between us *was* finished,' she returned, feeling strangely breathless.

'Not as far as I'm concerned,' he said evenly. 'And it won't be until I say so.' His features seemed even more predatory than she remembered. 'What makes you think you have the right to just disappear without trace?'

'Don't be ridiculous, Dane.' Even to her own ears her attempt at a laugh sounded shaky.

'Ridiculous?' He grabbed her by the arm, and she winced as his fingers dug cruelly into her tender flesh.

'Dane, for goodness' sake, you're hurting me!' She gazed up at him, genuinely astounded by his anger, yet equally taken aback to discover just how desperately she wanted to hurl herself into his arms. Agonising though this was, it was the first time she'd truly felt alive since leaving Glenshee.

'Not as much as I'd like to, lady,' he retorted grimly, his lips thinning to a cruel white line. 'How dare you run out on me?'

'Oh, is that it?' She felt her own temper rise, and welcomed it. 'You're mad because one of your conquests got away?' Sparks danced in her eyes as she squared up to him. 'What's wrong, Dane, did I hurt your macho pride by not sticking around for more? Well, I'm terribly sorry if I didn't add another notch to your bedpost, but look on the bright side—at least I saved you the bother of having to come up with a nice little farewell speech at the end of it all. I knew we'd made a mistake as soon as we'd. . .we'd. . .'

'Begun making love?' he supplied, a mocking little smile curving his lips. 'It's all right, Shannon, you won't burn in hell just because you dare to say the words.'

'We weren't making love,' she shot back at him. 'It was pure sex, and I should never have been so damn crazy! To think I nearly gave in to you!'

'Gave in to me?' His eyes mocked her. 'Now you sound like the wronged heroine in Victorian melodrama. Lady, as I recall there was no question of giving in on either side. You wanted me every bit as much as I wanted you.'

'It was nothing more than a mental aberration on my part.' Driven to fury by his goading and by her own uncontrollable reactions to him, Shannon all but spat the words. 'A moment's craziness, never to be repeated.'

Dane gripped her by the shoulders then, and she thought he would shake her. Instead he lifted his hands and pushed them deep into her hair, and, before she had time to get herself together, he was kissing her, his mouth hard and brutal against hers. She tried frantically to struggle, but his strength was far greater than hers, and even as she pushed against him she was overwhelmed by a far more desperate need to hold him, to feel his strong body pressed against hers once more. With an anguished whimper she gave up the fight and kissed him back with a fervour born of all the long, lonely nights she'd spent without him, her arms snaking up round his neck to pull him closer still. Feeling her surrender, his mouth gentled on hers and his fingers caressed her skin beneath her tousled hair.

'"A moment's craziness?"' He echoed her words of a few moments before, and the jarring note of triumph in his voice rang a warning bell somewhere in Shannon's mind. '"A mental aberration?"' His lip curled in a sneer, and a cold hand settled over her heart. 'Lady, I could have you any time I wanted to.'

She gazed at him in horrified disbelief as realisation hit home. 'You made the reservation for me at the hotel,' she said, forcing her voice to remain steady. 'And that's why that damned woman has been giving me such strange knowing looks! Is that why you've brought me here? To act as your personal bed-warmer?'

He stroked one long finger down her cheek, and she wondered savagely why, even now, she couldn't recoil from his touch.

'Perhaps,' he said.

She shook her head. 'Oh, no. I won't be your plaything, Dane Jacobsen. You may be responsible for my being here, but you can't make me stay.'

He raised one eyebrow mockingly. 'You'd walk out on a job, because of personal problems? Not a very professional attitude, Miss Shannon Lea.'

With a strength born of desperation, she wrenched herself out of his embrace, rage burning a slow fuse within her. He had her beaten and he knew it. He'd known perfectly well how she'd react when he'd arranged for her to be taken on for this play. He'd also known that when the chips were down she wouldn't back away.

'You've tricked me,' she said, her voice low and heavy. 'I'd never have come here if I'd known. . .'

'If you'd known I was here,' he finished the sentence calmly. 'I'm aware of that.'

'Why *are* you here?' she asked, suddenly curious. 'I'd have thought it would be the West End or nothing for Dane Jacobsen—superstar.' She eyed him coldly. 'Or is your star on the wane, finally?'

His lips thinned. 'Still the same little viper,' he said evenly. 'I'm here, Shannon Lea, because Josh Thayer, the playwright, is an old and valued friend of mine. He asked if I would do this play, and I agreed.'

She was unwillingly impressed. Actors of Dane's calibre didn't often do favours for unknown playwrights, no matter how old and valued their friendship. She wasn't about to let him see her reaction, though.

'How terribly sweet and noble of you,' she purred. 'I do hope Mr Thayer appreciates the great sacrifices you've made for him. Just think—you could be showing off your skiing prowess somewhere instead.'

A muscle twitched in his cheek, and she felt a strange sense of regret. She'd deliberately tried to antagonise him, and as usual she'd succeeded, so why couldn't she feel any pleasure in it? Because she was only doing it to protect herself, to hide the real truth—which was that she'd have given anything to simply thrown herself into his arms.

'How do you do it, Shannon?'

She flinched, fearful for a second that he'd read her mind. 'Do what?'

'How do you manage to contain two such totally different women inside one body?'

'I don't know what you mean.'

'Don't you?' The blue eyes seemed to bore into her, penetrating through the defensive layers she surrounded herself with. 'I think you do.'

She gave a careless shrug. 'What you see is what you get.'

'Oh, no.' He shook his head decisively. 'What I see is a beautiful, desirable woman. What I get. . .is a cold, unwelcoming ice-maiden. Except sometimes. . .' his eyes glittered strangely '. . .sometimes the ice-maiden forgets herself, and turns to flame in my arms. Which is the real you, Shannon Lea?'

She closed her eyes against the flicker of fear running through her veins. He was too perceptive, too intuitive, too dangerous. Sometimes she had the strangest feeling he knew her better than she knew herself, and if that were truly the case then how on earth was she to go on protecting herself? She was saved from answering by the sound of knocking at the door, and turned with relief to see Dane's face light up in welcome.

'Josh! Good to see you.' He slapped the other man on the shoulder, and Shannon studied him closely, curious to see the 'old and valued friend' for herself. Actually, he was more of a grizzly bear in human form—a short, solid man with a shaggy mane of hair and a full beard, and the twinkliest brown eyes anyone could ever imagine. Shannon couldn't help but feel a ripple of warmth for the man, even though they hadn't even been introduced yet. There was just something eminently likeable about him.

The same could not be said of his companion—a

tall, ravishing blonde with almond-shaped eyes and legs that went on forever, displayed to stunning effect in a little black figure-hugging dress that ended several inches above her knees. Beside her, in a pair of jeans and a comfortable sweatshirt, her hair tied back in a pony-tail, Shannon felt like a stable-hand.

'Shannon, I'd like you to meet the man I mentioned to you earlier, Josh Thayer, and this is Marianne McCall, our leading lady.'

Shannon held out her hand to both newcomers, wondering if it was simply her imagination that saw a coolly speculative gleam in Marianne's eyes. Certainly the actress seemed friendly enough, her perfectly carved mouth curving into a smile as she nodded amiably; yet there was something about her that sent a warning tingle up Shannon's spine.

'This is just like old times, eh, Dane?' She twined her arms round Dane's neck, planting a lingering kiss on his mouth, laughing huskily as she removed traces of her lipstick from his lips with her fingers. 'We've worked together before,' she told Shannon. 'What was it the last critic said, darling? Something about an incredible chemistry radiating between the two stars of the show?'

Dane smiled at her affectionately, and Shannon was horrified to feel jealousy stab like a dagger in her heart. Well, what could she expect? He was an incredibly handsome man, Marianne a stunningly attractive woman. Little wonder they'd created chemistry together.

'The same critic described the play as "a dog",' Dane reminded her wryly. 'If you recall, it closed after one night.'

Marianne's eyes narrowed a little, but her smile

never wavered. 'Still,' she purred provocatively, 'it was one sensational night.' Her glance slid to Shannon. 'And which part are you playing?'

'Shae's our make-up artist,' Dane cut in before Shannon had a chance to open her mouth.

Marianne laid a hand on his shoulder, giving him a playfully admonishing look. 'Really, darling, can't you let the girl answer for herself?' She cast a swift, assessing look over Shannon, her eyes giving nothing away. 'Will this be the first time you've worked in theatre?'

Shae shook her head. 'I've done a couple of shows. But mostly I've been working in television.'

'Another one lured by the small screen's filthy lucre.' Marianne looked up at Dane from beneath her ludicrously long eyelashes. 'What's the name of the thing you've been doing, my sweet? *The Norseman* or some such nonsense?'

'*The Viking*.' Dane smiled down at her fondly, though Shannon felt a severe prickle of aggravation on his behalf. He'd done good work on the drama pilot, and it was galling to hear this woman refer to it so dismissively. It was more irritating still to realise he wasn't in the least bit put out by the woman's comments. 'Shannon worked on the same production.'

'Did she, indeed?' For a split second the friendliness disappeared from Marianne's eyes to be replaced by a calculating glint. 'So you two know each other already—how sweet. Or is this reunion more than mere coincidence?' She looked slowly from one to the other, and it was Shannon who shook her head.

'No, it's not,' she said abruptly. 'I didn't know Mr

Jacobsen was in this play until I arrived here today.' That part, at least, was true.

Marianne appeared to consider that for a moment, then nodded. 'That must have been a nice surprise. For you both.'

'Hey, are we going to stand around here talking all day?' Josh cut in plaintively. 'I've been travelling for hours. I'm starving.'

Dane and Marianne exchanged a laughing, indulgent glance, seeming for all the world like two fond parents, and Shae looked away, all too aware that she was being excluded from the charmed circle.

'Come on, then,' Dane said. 'We might as well all go and find a restaurant.'

'I'll pass, if you don't mind,' Shae cut in. 'I'd like to get an early night, so I'll just grab a sandwich back at the hotel.'

'Nonsense.' Josh tucked his arm companionably through hers. 'You and I have got some serious talking to do—I'm not about to let the director have things all his own way where make-up's concerned. I know my characters better than he does. Now, have you had a chance to think about Dane's character yet?' He was still talking as he propelled her through the door and back along the corridor towards the exit, barely pausing for breath, and giving her no chance at all to interrupt.

They made their way to the hotel car park, where Dane's distinctive white BMW was parked, Marianne chatting non-stop as they went in her low, husky voice. Shannon knew she was being excluded from the conversation, though there was absolutely no evidence of that. She gave herself a mental shake; Marianne was simply like many other egocentric actresses she'd met—interested more in herself than in anything else—but that didn't necessarily mean she was trying to shut Shannon out. Why should she? Shae was hardly competition. She was letting her imagination run away with her.

'Sharon, sweetheart, I hope you won't mind terribly if I take the passenger seat?' Marianne turned beseeching green eyes on Shae. 'I know it's silly, but I've never outgrown a childhood tendency to travel sickness. It's never as bad if I can travel in the front of the car.'

'I don't mind at all,' Shannon returned evenly, only just managing to stifle a grin as she caught sight of Josh rolling his eyes.

'It's just as well you remember your lines more accurately than you remember people's names,' he cut in drily. 'The young lady's name is Shannon, not Sharon.'

Marianne settled herself comfortably beside Dane, and turned with an apologetic little smile. 'How silly of me,' she said sweetly. 'And yours is such a charming name, too. Are your people Irish?'

Shae shook her head. 'I come from a small village in the far north of Scotland.'

'But how delightful!' Marianne returned. 'Then visiting a big city must be exciting for you.'

'I have seen a few busy streets in my life,' Shae said quietly, sure she was being baited, but refusing to let herself rise to it.

'Has most of your work been in Scotland?'

Shannon named the television station where she'd worked before turning freelance, and the other woman pursed her lips thoughtfully.

'How interesting.'

Then she turned back to Dane, effectively ending the audience, and for the rest of the trip her conversation was reserved for the driver alone. Josh turned towards Shae, lowering his voice conspiratorially.

'Don't pay any attention,' he advised. 'It's always the same when they get together; Marianne considers Dane her exclusive property. She likes to monopolise him whenever she gets the chance.'

Shannon managed to smile, wondering why Josh had felt it necessary to explain. Had Dane told him about the weekend in Glenshee? The thought chilled her.

'It's all right,' she murmured. 'They must have a lot of catching up to do.'

For the rest of the trip there might as well have been a sound-proof grill between the front and back seats, Shannon reflected wryly. Admittedly Dane did throw the odd comment over his shoulder as they drove, pointing out places of interest, but every time he did so Marianne managed to draw his attention back by launching into yet another anecdote which involved only herself and Dane.

Later they found a small, quiet restaurant on the outskirts of the city, and Shannon couldn't help but notice the admiring glances of male diners and waiters as Marianne swayed into the room. It wasn't that the actress actually did anything to attract attention, she acknowledged grudgingly—with those looks and that centrefold body, she didn't need to. When they were shown to a table in a side-booth, Marianne slid in beside Dane, then looked at Shae with a cool little smile.

'I'm sorry, did you want to sit here?'

Shannon shook her head. 'This seat's fine.'

They ordered dinner, then conversation turned to the play, and for once Marianne lost centre stage as Josh began talking about his own work and the hopes he had for it.

'You know the play's set in the twenty-first century,' Josh explained. 'Dane plays the space-station commander—a figure of authority, but one who's all too prone to human frailty. I suppose in a way you could draw parallels with the old Samson and Delilah story,' he said, leaning forward in his seat to make his point. 'The temptress in this case, however, is——'

'Me.' Marianne bestowed a smouldering look on Dane, her green eyes slanting provocatively, and Shannon felt her stomach muscles clench. How could any red-blooded male ignore the message the actress was sending so blatantly? she wondered despairingly. And if he wasn't tempted now, how could he possibly act out his role on stage night after night without being affected? With an effort she kept her eyes away from Dane, knowing she couldn't bear to see answering desire for Marianne in his face.

'Save it for the audience,' Josh said drily, his friendly brown eyes faintly annoyed as he took in the scene. 'You don't need to start rehearsals yet, Marianne.'

'Who said I was rehearsing?' She pouted prettily at the playwright. 'Dane and I hardly need to practise passion.' She slid a look at Shae, who managed with an effort to keep her own all-too expressive features bland.

'Well, rehearsals proper start tomorrow.' Josh glanced at his watch with a grimace. 'And I, for one, would like a good night's sleep before the chaos begins. Shall we return to the hotel?'

Dane pulled his car-keys from his pocket and handed them across the table.

'I'd like to walk back,' he said. 'I could do with a breath of fresh air.'

'I'll walk with you,' Marianne offered promptly, but Josh firmly shook his head.

'There's a couple of things I'd like to talk over with you before tomorrow,' he said. 'Come back with me in the car, and we'll have a chat.'

Irritation flashed briefly in the beautiful green eyes, but was quickly replaced by a beaming smile.

'Of course, Josh. It'll do Dane good to be alone for a little while. After all, he and I will be practically inseparable after tonight—to help us really get into the skins of our stage characters.' The look she cast across the table said clearly that she personally intended to make sure that was the case, and Shannon felt a strange little shiver in her spine. Marianne McCall might be hiding her true colours from the men, but it seemed she felt no need to do the same where Shae was concerned. It was as if she'd thrown down an invisible gauntlet on the table, and Shae knew a moment's bleakness. If the gorgeous actress really had set her sights on Dane, and it seemed she had, he probably wouldn't even want to resist.

'I wasn't intending to walk alone,' Dane said quietly. 'Want to take an evening stroll, Shae?'

She should have said no. Being alone with him, even on busy city streets, could turn out to be more than she could bear. But even as she began to shake her head, she heard her own voice accepting the invitation, felt a ridiculous little spurt of pleasure that he even wanted to be with her.

'Well——' Marianne shook her blonde hair back

over her shoulder '—you know which room I'm in, Dane. If you want to see me later. . .' Shc touched her fingers to her lips and blew him a kiss, laughing huskily. 'Just don't leave it too late. I'd like to get *some* sleep tonight.'

He smiled back at her, and the knife twisted still deeper in Shae's stomach, robbing her of the pleasure of just a moment ago. What was she doing here? Why hadn't she simply walked out of the theatre as soon as she'd discovered he was in the cast?

The thought kept her silent as she walked along beside him, forced to quicken her steps to keep up with his long-legged strides. And why had he persuaded the director to hire her? None of this made any sense—none of it. It should all have ended with her escape from Glenshee; why was he doing this to her? When they reached the hotel, he walked with her to her room, and she thanked him in a rather stilted voice for a very pleasant evening.

'You're more than welcome, Miss Lea.' His lips quirked at the corners in ill-disguised amusement.

'Have you known Marianne for long?' She strove to keep her tone casual, offhand.

He gave a low chuckle. 'Years. We were in the same drama class.'

'You seem—very close.'

He glanced at her questioningly. 'Is that an oblique way of asking me just how close?'

She gave a tiny shrug, hating the weakness in herself that pushed her to probe for details. 'It's really none of my business.'

He nodded. 'You're right. It isn't.'

She was both saddened and angered by his terse answer. Just what was he trying to do to her? She was only here because he'd manoeuvred it; now he seemed determined to keep her at arm's length. What did it all mean?

She gave a tiny sigh. 'I'm tired, Dane. I'm going to bed.'

He took her room key from her and slid it into the lock, and she felt suddenly breathless. Had he taken her words as an invitation? Did he intend to enter the room with her? Only too aware that her bed was just a few feet away, she gazed up at him, her eyes showing her confusion.

He smiled mirthlessly. 'Don't bother with the frightened-fawn act, Shannon Lea. I'm not about to fulfil your fantasies by sweeping you off your feet and into bed.'

'*My* fantasies?' The confusion fled, quickly replaced by sheer disbelief. 'What are you talking about?'

He moved closer, pinning her up against the door. 'I don't think I need to spell it out to you, my frightened little virgin,' he said in a voice that was soft yet laden with scorn. 'I saw the way you looked at Marianne tonight; you don't like her, do you? You don't like her because she's a woman who's not afraid to show what she wants.'

'You're being ridiculous,' Shannon returned shakily, horribly aware of his nearness.

'I think not.' His eyes were cool with contempt. 'I think you want exactly the same things she does, but you hide behind the pillars of your ice palace, pretending to be so unapproachable. And what would you do if someone were to break down those pillars, Shae—scream and protest and say it had all been done against your will?'

He was so close now she could barely breathe, could feel his warm breath on her skin.

'You could never break them down,' she said with tremulous bravado.

'No?' He raised a disbelieving eyebrow. 'Think again, Shannon Lea.' His head dipped towards her, and she braced herself for another of his harsh, punishing kisses, knowing any attempt at escape would be a complete waste of time. But when his lips touched hers they were soft, caressing, and her knees nearly buckled beneath her. Her mouth opened of its own free will to his playfully probing tongue, welcoming the invader. In his arms, pressed close against the hard, powerful body she'd never been able to banish from her mind, she forgot everything but him, knew nothing but the agonising joy of being in his arms. His hand slipped upwards from her waist, and anticipation of his touch on her breasts made the breath catch in her throat. Then, abruptly, his mouth left her, and she gazed up at him in confused distress, her body still longing for his caress.

'You have a sweet, giving body, Shannon,' he said. 'When I touch you, you're unable to deny me anything.' His eyes narrowed coldly. 'Pity that body houses such a closed-in mind.'

He pushed away from her, and she was forced to lean against the door, shaken by the strength of the desire he'd sent coursing through her, horrified by her own weakness. He walked away down the corridor, without so much as a backward look, and tears stung her eyes. He was going to Marianne—to a woman who'd welcome him with both body and mind. A woman who wasn't afraid to love.

CHAPTER SIX

REHEARSALS began the following day, plunging Shannon into a hectic whirlwind of activity that seemed to have no let-up as the week progressed, but she was glad of it—glad of the work that kept her mind as well as her hands busy. She wasn't too busy, however, to notice that Marianne kept her promise, monopolising Dane whenever she could, finding countless reasons to draw him away from whatever he was doing. Not that he seemed to mind in the slightest, she acknowledged wryly, forced to bite her lips in silence every time the actress materialised apparently from nowhere to spirit Dane away.

She landed up with still more work on her hands when the wardrobe mistress fell ill and she found herself gamely stepping into the breach.

'I'm afraid this tunic is a little on the tight side,' she told Marianne at the first fitting of her costume, after tugging ineffectually at the zip on the shimmery silver material. 'I'll let the seams out a little.'

'Are you suggesting I'm too fat?' Alone with Shannon, Marianne didn't bother to keep up the saccharin-sweet condescension she bestowed on her when Dane and Josh were around, and the undisguised venom in her green eyes sent a ripple of unease along Shae's spine.

'I wasn't suggesting anything of the sort,' Shae returned evenly. 'But you don't want to be uncomfortable on stage.'

'I suppose you'd rather I was clothed in a voluminous sack; then your beloved Dane wouldn't be able to ogle my body as he normally does.'

Mentally counting to ten, Shannon gripped the zipper firmly and hauled it up.

'There,' she said, making a deliberate attempt to keep her expression bland. 'How's that?'

'Perfect.' Marianne surveyed her reflection in the mirror, her eyes gleaming in satisfaction as they swept over her own generous curves, clearly outlined by the skin-tight material. 'I should think Dane will enjoy embracing me in this outfit, don't you?'

Shannon managed a smile, refusing to let the woman see she was affected in any way by her taunting.

'I should think any man would,' she returned quietly.

'But Dane Jacobsen isn't just any man.' Marianne's green eyes were blatantly challenging. 'And I should know that better than anyone. After all we've been to one another in the past. . .' She let her words trail away, and, even though she knew exactly what the actress was trying to do, Shae felt the sharp niggle of acid jealousy deep in the pit of her stomach. Biting her lips, she turned away, pretending to busy herself with one of the other costumes.

'Tell me, Shannon, just what exactly is there between you and Dane?'

With her back still turned to Marianne, Shae frowned, puzzled. Why did she need to know? Wasn't it enough for her that she had Dane, while Shae slept alone every night?

'Surely if you're so close you should know the

answer to that,' she said at last, mentally awarding herself a point for her own coolness.

'He and I don't spend our time talking trivia.' Marianne tossed her long blonde hair contemptuously, and Shae wryly deducted the point. Unaccustomed to waging this kind of war, she was no match for the other woman's powers of cattiness.

'If it's so trivial, then there's no need for you to know the answer.'

Marianne shrugged offhandedly. 'No need at all, except to offer a friendly word of advice.'

Biting back the answer she'd have liked to make, Shannon raised her eyebrows expectantly. 'Advice?'

'Yes.' The green eyes narrowed calculatingly. 'I've seen the way you look at him—and frankly we've all found it rather embarrassing to see the lovesick look on your face whenever he's anywhere near you. At least have the dignity to keep your feelings to yourself.' She picked up a brush from the dressing-table and began sweeping it through her thick, luxuriant hair. 'He won't tell you himself, of course—he's too nice for that. In fact, ever since I've known him he's had a penchant for adopting stray dogs. But it must be tiresome for him to have you constantly tagging at his heels all the time.' She laid down the brush and faced Shae directly. 'So why don't you give him a break? He'd far rather be with the grown-ups then playing nursemaid to you.'

Her words sliced through Shannon like burning arrows, but only a faint staining of her cheeks showed she'd been affected in the slightest. She had to call on acting powers she'd never known she possessed to face Marianne calmly, but before she could say a word there was a knock on the door and Josh's friendly, bearded face appeared.

'Hope I'm not interrupting anything,' he said. 'The director wants to see you right away, Marianne, and Dane asked me to tell you he'll be down in just a few minutes, Shae, to finish off his costume fitting.' The brown eyes twinkled fondly. 'If you ask me, he simply wants a few moments in sane and pleasant company, away from the madhouse.' He glanced at Marianne, frowning slightly. 'That costume's too tight. It shows every bulge.' He winked at Shannon, then closed the door behind him as Marianne turned angrily from the mirror.

'Don't be fooled by that,' she snapped. 'He may have some kind of interest in you for the moment, little make-up lady, but, believe me, it won't last. He's had his meaningless little flings before—but he always comes back to me in the end. Your sweet, milk-sop charms may be attracting him now, but it takes a woman to hold him. A *real* woman.'

Only the rigidity of Shannon's spine betrayed the tension in her body as she gave a slight nod.

'We'll just have to see, won't we?' she returned neutrally.

Only when Marianne swept from the room did she allow herself to collapse into a chair, closing her eyes and rubbing her fingers over her forehead. Maintaining that calm, uncaring façade even for just a few minutes had taken a lot out of her, and she felt the faint beginnings of a headache behind her eyes. The worst thing was knowing Marianne was right. She'd wondered all along why someone like Dane should be attracted to her. Surrounded as he was by the glamour of the acting world, he could pick and choose from the world's most beautiful women—women like Marianne, with her lush body and provocative, slanting green eyes.

Maybe he'd brought her here to act as some kind of pawn in a game he played with Marianne, she realised dully. He'd avoided giving her a direct answer when she'd tried to ask him about his friendship with the actress, but it was obvious that there was a very real chemistry between them. Their love scenes on stage were too real, too convincing to be purely make-believe.

'Taking a breather?'

Startled, she looked up into Dane's sea-blue eyes, and even as she tried to strengthen herself against him she felt a rush of longing so intense that it made her weak at the knees. Would he always have this effect on her?

'Something like that,' she murmured. 'It's been a hectic day.'

He nodded. 'This is the first opportunity I've had to get away from Josh and the director. But now they're having a heated debate about script changes, so I grabbed the chance to escape for a few minutes.'

'Did you want something?' She rose slowly to her feet.

His features darkened. 'Are you this welcoming to everyone who comes in?' Without waiting for her answer, he made a dismissive gesture. 'Never mind. I want to try on my costume. Is it ready?'

She nodded. 'I'll take it through to your dressing-room.'

'Don't bother. I'll try it on here.'

'Then I'll wait outside.'

His lips curled scornfully. 'What's wrong, Shae?

Scared of seeing my unclothed body?' He took a step towards her as he started to unbutton his shirt, and she forced herself not to give him the satisfaction of moving away. 'You've seen me naked before,' he continued, his voice soft yet laden with some kind of threat. 'You've lain with me, in my arms, your skin against my skin.'

'Stop it!' She lifted her eyes to search his face. 'Why are you doing this? Why can't you just leave me alone?'

'You can't stand it, can you?' He shrugged the shirt from his broad shoulders and threw it casually on to a chair. 'You can't stand the fact that I know what you're really like behind that ice-cool façade.'

'You don't know me at all,' she spat back.

He raised one eyebrow mockingly. 'No?' He lifted her nerveless hand and held it palm down against his own naked chest. Even that slight contact sent a shudder through her body, but she fought it, refusing to let him see how he could move her. 'I think I do, Shannon Lea; I know that, much as you like to play the frightened virgin, there's a passionate woman inside of you, desperate to emerge.' His free hand snaked round her waist, and she gasped as he pulled her hard against him. 'I also know I'm the only one capable of freeing that butterfly from its crysalis.'

'How dare you?' She tried to wrench free, but he held her effortlessly, smiling coldly as he stroked her hand over his own chest. Infuriated by his physical superiority, she curved her fingers inward, digging her nails into his skin.

'So the little kitten has claws,' he murmured. 'Good. I prefer women with spirit.'

'Then go to Marianne,' Shae spat savagely. 'She

surely has spirit enough to satisfy you. Or has she outlived her usefulness?'

He smiled. 'Are you jealous of her, Shannon Lea?'

'No!' She all but screamed the denial, horribly aware that it wasn't true. 'If she's fool enough to want you, she can have you. I'd be happy if I never had to set eyes on you again!'

'Liar.' There was no anger in his voice, simply mocking amusement. 'The truth is, it tears you apart to think of me being with Marianne night after night, making love to her, holding her in my arms the way I once held you.' He lowered his head, murmuring into her hair, and she closed her eyes, helpless against the softly insistent power of his voice.

'Why are you doing this?' she murmured brokenly. 'You don't need me.'

'But I want you,' he said. 'And I will have you.'

'Never.' She poured her soul into that one word, but he just shook his head.

'The battle's already lost,' he said. 'After all, I have the greatest ally of all on my side.'

'Meaning?' She raised her eyes to his.

'Meaning—no matter what sort of games your mind wants to play, your body wants me. And it will win in the end.' He drew the splayed fingers of one hand over her throat and down to cup one breast, and, even as she tried to back away, Shannon felt her nipples puckering, begging for his touch. He smiled. 'You see, Shannon? Bodies don't tell lies.'

She threw her head back, her sherry-coloured eyes ablaze with defiance. 'Bodies have no powers of reasoning,' she said through gritted teeth. 'They feel and display desire—lust, even. If my body responds to you, it means nothing, nothing at all!'

His hand slid over her breast to sweep the curve of her narrow waist, then settled on her hip, and she closed her eyes against the river of heat his touch sent coursing through her veins.

'And does your body respond to any other man this way?' he said softly. 'Has it ever hungered like this for the caress of any other lover?'

She swayed helplessly against him, held captive by the spell of his hands and his hypnotically persuasive voice. Barely realising what she was doing, she ran her fingers over his chest, loving the feel of the thick, silky mat of hair.

'Answer me, Shannon.'

She shook her head, unable to ignore his command. 'No, damn you!' she cried. 'But you're an experienced man—you've made love to many, many women. How could I hope to remain unmoved?'

He tilted her chin upwards, forcing her to look into his predatory hawklike features, his thumb rubbing against the fullness of her lower lip.

'That's not it, Shannon Lea,' he said quietly. 'You're lying to yourself again if you think your response is purely a result of my skill.' His eyes held her ensnared. 'I could look at you across a room full of people, and still make you weak with longing.'

'My God, you're insufferable,' she shot back. 'You believe yourself invincible—irresistible!'

Infuriated by his arrogance, she tried to wrench herself free, but he was ready for her, holding her with no visible effort.

'You try to defend yourself with words, but they are empty, meaningless,' he said. 'Do you know why? Because you are mine, Shannon. You belong to me.'

'Never! I belong to no one but myself.'

He smiled. 'I can wait, my little spitfire. I can wait until you come to me, willingly, gladly, of your own free will.'

'Then you'll wait forever.'

He slanted her a thoughtfully challenging look. 'Are you really so sure your defences against me are inviolable?'

'Certain,' she returned, with more than a touch of bravado.

'Then prove it.'

'I beg your pardon?' She frowned, puzzled by his sudden change of tack.

'You heard me, Shannon. Prove to me—and perhaps to yourself, too, that you can be with me and remain unmoved.'

Still held in the circle of his arms, Shae unconsciously squared her shoulders, preparing for the impossible challenge.

'How?'

He gave a slight shrug. 'Nothing very difficult. Come out with me tonight—not with the rest of the theatre crowd, but alone.'

She eyed him suspiciously. 'Why?'

An amused smile played at the corners of his mouth. 'Why not? Does the idea make you afraid?'

If truth were told, it made her a lot more than simply afraid, but telling him that would simply add to his ammunition.

'Don't be ridiculous,' she said shortly. 'Very well, Dane, I will go out with you. Just as I would with any other male acquaintance.'

His lips quirked at the description, but he made no comment on her careful choice of words.

'Fine. I'll meet you in the hotel foyer.'

He dipped his head towards her, and for a breathless moment she thought he was about to kiss her. Despite everything she'd said, her eyes fluttered closed in unspoken invitation, but at the last second she heard his laughter, low and mocking.

'Tonight, Shannon Lea. Tonight.'

Shannon sat down on the bed with a despairing thump. What on earth was she supposed to wear for this evening with Dane—this evening that wasn't exactly a date, yet she could think of no other description for it? She'd rifled through the contents of her wardrobe twice, groaning disgustedly as she discounted one garment after another. It was ridiculous, of course; by rights she should have been perfectly happy to throw on any old thing, the more unflattering the better, since the whole purpose of the exercise was to convince Dane she didn't want him. But pride wouldn't let her do that—pride insisted she at least made an effort.

She caught sight of her own reflection in the mirror and uttered a single soft curse. Pride be damned! There was no point in trying to delude herself. She wanted to look good for Dane because she was responding to the age-old instinct of women everywhere who felt the need to dress up and be beautiful for their men.

'But he's *not* my man!' She gripped her hands together fiercely, as though she could force the words into her brain. 'He's nothing to me, nothing!'

And God didn't make little green apples, she thought, feeling an almost hysterical desire to laugh, though the situation was anything but amusing. She threw herself off the bed and hauled the first outfit that came to hand from the wardrobe. Getting through this evening would be hard enough in itself without driving herself crazy over deciding what to wear. A short while later she glanced in the mirror, seeing a small, slender figure dressed in a mid-calf-length denim skirt, cuban-heeled cowboy-boots and white fringed shirt, her riotous auburn curls left tumbling free over her shoulders. All she needed was a pair of shooters slung from her hip and she'd be little Annie Oakley, she thought derisively, reaching instead for her favourite Navajo belt. Well, at least no one could accuse her of dressing provacatively—it was hardly an outfit that would knock anyone's eyes out.

Despite that, Dane's eyes glinted appreciatively when she joined him in the hotel foyer, and to her annoyance she felt a pleasant little warm glow deep inside.

'Very pretty,' he said. 'I think this is the first time I've seen you in anything but jeans or salopettes.' Then he smiled archly. 'Except for one other memorable occasion, of course—when you were wearing nothing at all.'

Her cheeks flamed with fierce heat at the memory, and she scowled at him.

'I'd rather forget that ever happened,' she snapped.

He shrugged. 'As you wish. Shall we go?'

Miserably aware that the evening had lurched off to a regrettable start, Shannon fell into step beside him, irritated still further when she caught the receptionist's knowing smirk at the sight of them walking out together.

'That woman thinks we're sleeping together,' she said in an undertone.

'Woman?' Dane glanced down at her with a frown.

'The receptionist. She's been giving me strange looks ever since I got here—doubtless because it's not exactly commonplace for the star of the show to make bookings for the lowly make-up artist.'

He shook his head exasperatedly. 'Don't you think you're becoming a little paranoid, Shae? If you were sleeping with me, I'd have booked a double room. I don't play childish hide-and-seek games.'

'She doesn't know that.'

'She doesn't need to. What I do—and who I do it with—is very much my own business.'

Shae lapsed into silence as they walked along the road together. It was easy for him; the cloak of arrogance he habitually wore probably made him oblivious to the speculation of people like the receptionist. Even if he were aware of it, he probably wouldn't care in the slightest. Shae was made of different stuff; in his company she felt as though she were walking under a permanent spotlight, and the awareness of questioning eyes upon her made her deeply uncomfortable. That was undoubtedly a legacy of her childhood, she thought resignedly—a throwback to the days when she and her mother had been forced to hold their heads high and attempt to ignore the pointing fingers. Her mother had succeeded. Shae hadn't always.

'This will do.'

She blinked, so deep in thought that his voice took her by surpirse.

'I beg your pardon?'

He nodded impatiently towards a small, cosy-looking pub. 'I said this will do. We'll go in here.'

With a conscious effort, she swallowed the small spurt of irritation against his easy presumption that she'd simply fall into line with whatever he chose to do.

'Fine.'

He rewarded her with a cool smile as they entered the pub, and gestured towards a table. 'I'll get the drinks.'

Without even bothering to ask what she wanted to drink, she bridled inwardly. Really, the man was impossible. The autocratic streak ran so strong in him that he probably didn't even realise he was being high-handed. Well, for tonight she'd play the game by his rules—up to a certain point. But he'd discover she wasn't the malleable little miss, if he tried to push her too far.

'What did you tell Marianne you were doing tonight?' she asked as he returned with the drinks.

'Why should I tell her anything?'

She gave a little shrug. 'I thought you and she——'

'I didn't bring you here to talk about my relationship with Marianne,' he cut in brusquely. 'As far as you're concerned, the subject's off-limits.'

'Well, I beg your pardon!' High colour leapt to her cheeks as anger danced in her tawny eyes. 'Heaven forbid that I should dare to question anything you would do.' She bit her bottom lip. 'Do you impose the same rules on her?'

'Meaning?'

'Meaning—do you slap her down if she dares to ask about the other women in your life?'

There was little warmth in his answering smile. 'She knows better than to ask.' He regarded her steadily across the table. 'What about you, Shannon Lea?'

She stiffened automatically. 'What about me?'

'Something about you suggests you've never been deeply involved in a relationship,' he mused, seeming almost to be speaking to himself rather than to her. 'You remind me of a wild animal sometimes, poised ready to flee at the first sight of a hunter's gun.'

'Perhaps because I don't wish to be shot.' Her attempt at a light laugh didn't quite make it.

'Hunters don't always want to shoot their prey,' he returned softly. 'Sometimes capture is enough.'

'Then I've never wished to be captured,' she returned bluntly. 'I've seen what can happen when a person loses their heart—and their freedom—to someone else.'

He nodded thoughtfully. 'Is that why you flew from me after that night in Glenshee?'

The directness of the question startled her, and for a moment she was lost for an answer. To tell him the truth—that she'd been afraid of the depth of her own feelings—would be far too revealing. Yet what other answer could she give? For a moment she considered saying nothing at all—after all, he had refused to answer her questions. However, the steely look in his blue eyes told her such tactics would be ultimately pointless, and she sighed heavily.

'I was confused.' She dropped her eyes to study the contents of her glass. 'Everything was happening so fast.'

'It was your first time, wasn't it?'

She frowned, not understanding at first, then felt a faint flush steal into her cheeks as his meaning became clear.

'I am a virgin, yes,' she said stiltedly. 'Ridiculous,

isn't it, in this day and age to find a twenty-seven-year-old virgin? But there it is.'

She felt the unexpected warmth of his fingers against her cheek, and looked up, startled.

'There's nothing ridiculous about it,' he said quietly. 'Do you regret what happened between us?'

The question made Shannon smile. She might rue the night for many reasons, but deep down she could never regret being part of something so beautiful.

'No,' she returned softly. 'No, I don't regret it.'

For a long moment they gazed silently into each other's eyes, and she felt the familiar tug of longing deep in her stomach. A distant part of her mind wondered if she'd ever be able to look at this man and not want him, but in truth she already knew the answer. He was emblazoned on her heart, a part of her very soul.

'Dane, I. . .'

'Well, well, look who's here!'

The moment was abruptly shattered by the sound of Marianne's distinctive husky voice. As Shannon looked up she caught a coldly calculating glint in the actress's green eyes, but it was gone before Marianne turned to Dane, her beautifully shaped mouth pouting prettily.

'You should have told me you were coming out, darling—I'd have kept you company.'

'Hello, Marianne.' There was more than a touch of irritation in Dane's voice. 'How did you find us?'

'Find you?' She raised her eyebrows in well-affected surprise. 'I didn't set out to find you—it's sheer coincidence that I should chance to walk along the same street and into the same pub. But as I'm here, it seems a shame to let this spare seat go to waste,' she continued blithely. 'Move along a little, Dane, darling. There's plenty of room for me beside you.' She glanced over at Shannon. 'How sweet you look tonight! I remember when the wild-west look was in fashion, though I must confess I never really cared for it myself.'

Dane shot Shae a wry grimace, and she smiled resignedly. For a little while she'd almost managed to forget about Marianne., She should have known the other woman wouldn't allow that to remain the case for very long.

CHAPTER SEVEN

'SO MUCH for our evening alone.' Dane smiled a little ruefully down at Shae as they stood outside her bedroom door. 'Things weren't supposed to turn out that way.'

She shook her head. 'Don't worry. I enjoyed the evening.' Or would have but for the poisonous Marianne, she added silently. Deeply as she disliked and distrusted the actress, she still wasn't certain just how Dane felt about her, and she wasn't about to pin her own colours to the mast and risk having him leap to the other woman's defence. This evening, after his initial annoyance at her intrustion, he'd apparently enjoyed her company, laughing and joking along with her as she recounted ever more risqué stories in that sultry, husky voice of hers. Shae had laughed too, but it had been an effort, most of all because he'd never relaxed like that in her company.

She looked away from Dane's eyes now, suddenly gripped by an almost overwhelming need to ask him to stay. Standing there so close, she could smell the unmistakably male fragrance of him, a scent so heady that it almost made her sway towards him. Will-power alone kept her rigidly in place. She wasn't even sure just why he was there—they'd left Marianne in the hotel lounge downstairs with some of the other actors, but that didn't mean she wouldn't be joining him in his room later.

'Well,' she said quietly, steeling herself to say the words, 'I'll wish you goodnight.'

He gave a low, knowing chuckle. 'You're sending me to my lonely bed?'

She winced, wondering just what game he was playing now. She knew only too well that his bed probably wouldn't be empty; was he so desperately in need of fresh conquests that he would attempt to seduce Shae while Marianne kicked her heels downstairs, awaiting her turn?

'It's been a long day, Dane.'

But even as she made to turn away, his arms slid around her and she closed her eyes to everything but the sheer beauty of his kiss, the exquisite torture of his lips moving over her own, the hard strength of his body pressed against hers. Suddenly a low, mocking laugh rang out in the corridor, and she jumped as though she'd been shot, her heart racing as she looked round into scornful green eyes.

'Oh, come, children.' Marianne swayed provocatively towards them, her lush figure and endless legs shown off to perfection in a body-hugging mini-dress. 'Surely you're beyond the stage of stealing kisses behind the bicycle sheds?'

Shannon's cheeks flamed, and Marianne laughed scornfully.

'Look, Dane, how terribly sweet—a woman who can still blush!' She laid a hand on Shannon's arm. 'I really shouldn't tease. It's just such a rarity to find someone so—so innocent these days. And particularly in Dane Jacobsen's company!' She slid Dane a coquettish glance from beneath heavy black eyelashes. 'Or is that the real secret behind this unlikely attraction? Have you fallen for the coy-virgin act, my darling? Is it a case of wanting what you think you can't have?' She rolled her eyes heavenwards. 'Well, in this day and age that approach does at least have the benefit of novelty, I'll grant you that, Shannon, my dear.' She patted Shae comfortingly on the shoulder, while her eyes flashed pure malevolence. 'But, if I know him, you won't remain so charmingly ingenuous for long, so I'd make the most of it if I were you.'

She reached up to plant a light kiss on Dane's mouth. 'You know where I am when you tire of the game, my sweet. I'll be waiting.' She walked away along the corridor with the sinuous grace of a cat—an alley-cat, Shae thought, with a sudden savagery that took her by surprise.

'What did she mean by that?' she asked in a low voice.

'By what?' Dane stroked a strand of hair back from her flushed cheek.

'That I wouldn't remain so "charmingly ingenuous for long"?' Feeling an inexplicable pain in her chest, she gazed at him accusingly. 'Do you make a habit of corrupting women? Am I simply the latest victim in a long line?'

'I don't corrupt women,' he returned evenly, but with a hint of tightly controlled anger.

'But you've robbed quite a number of their innocence.'

The sea-blue eyes narrowed dangerously. 'I've never been a monk, Shannon. But I've never taken a woman against her will.'

'No, you wouldn't have to, would you?' Acid rose in her throat and, even though she knew her anger was, in truth, directed at Marianne, she couldn't prevent it from spilling into her words. 'The great and beautiful Dane Jacobsen would merely have to cock a finger and the object of his desires would surely come running.' She glared at him, bitterness clear in her eyes. 'Is that what made me different? The fact that I tried to get away from you—presented you with an unaccustomed challenge?'

She turned to the door and flung it open with one comtemptuous move. 'Well, let's get it over with. You said you'd wait till I came to you of my own free will; let's not prolong the agony any longer. You'll soon have your fill of me, after all—the little innocent from the middle of nowhere. Then you can return to rather more exotic fare—like the willing and voluptuous Marianne. Well, what are you waiting for?'

A cruel, mocking smile curved his lips, and he took a couple of steps towards her. Suddenly afraid of what she had unleashed, Shae backed away, barely realising she'd stepped into her own room till he closed the door behind them.

'What now?' she snapped, apprehension putting her on the attack. 'Are you about to forget all your fine words and simply take what you want?'

'You're forgetting, Miss Lea,' he murmured in a soft voice that made her shiver, 'you invited me in.'

'I've changed my mind.' She made a move to dodge past him, but his hand snaked out, catching her wrist in a vice-like grip that made her cry out. She tried to twist free, but in one deft movement he hooked his arm beneath her knees and, completely oblivious to her struggles, threw her on to the bed. Frantically Shannon tried to wriggle away, but he was too fast for her, his large body effectively pinning her to the mattress, and when she tried to slap him he caught her flailing wrists and held them fast on the pillow above her head.

'You said you'd never forced a woman,' she spat savagely, painfully aware of the way her breasts were jutting against him.

In his eyes there was no warmth, just cool, masculine arrogance.

'As you said yourself, Miss Lea—I've never had to.' Then his head dipped towards her and he kissed her full on the lips, a harsh, plundering kiss that robbed her of breath and left her trembling beneath him.

'Dane,' she commanded shakily, 'you must stop this.'

He ignored her words, capturing her mouth with his own again, his lips moving over hers with a sensual expertise that took her breath away. Even as she recognised the skill behind the caress, she was jolted by a dart of sheer untrammelled longing deep within her, and, hard as she tried to fight her own traitorous desires, she knew she was lost. Obviously aware of the moment when he'd won the battle, Dane released her hands, and her arms slid of their own accord round his back, pulling him closer still, as if suddenly she couldn't get enough of him.

His hands slid down her body, making her moan as they traced the shape of her breasts, his thumbs flickering over her hardening nipples through the thin cotton of her shirt. Deftly he undid the buttons and impatiently pushed the material back, his fingers sending tongues of fire through her body as he caressed her naked skin. He buried his face against her throat, his mouth tormenting her with its lazy progress down towards the swell of her breasts, and she arched up, silently begging for his caress.

He laughed deep in his throat, and, even as a tiny part of her rebelled against the triumphant sound, it dissolved into nothing as his mouth closed over one nipple, his tongue flicking lazily over the hard bud. His hand stroked along her leg, his touch burning even through the denim of her skirt, and she groaned in an agony of longing. She felt her skirt being tugged upwards, then his fingers, warm and possessive on the soft skin of her thigh, turned her to liquid. She was powerless to resist him, helpless against the torrent of passion building up within her as his questing fingers slid relentlessly towards the very centre of her desire. There was nothing she could do to stop what must surely now be inevitable, and part of her gloried in the surrender.

Then his weight lifted and she opened her dazed eyes, confused, as he moved away to sit at the edge of the bed.

'Dane, I. . .'

He shook his head, stilling her words.

'I think I've made my point,' he said evenly. 'I will have what's mine, Shannon Lea—but I won't take it. I'll wait till it's freely given.'

After all that had just happened, his apparent lack of emotion was impossible to bear, and a wave of anger washed over her.

'How dare you?' she cried. 'How dare you push your way in here and attempt to force me. . .?'

'Force, Shannon?' Dane's mocking eyes flickered lazily over her dishevelled clothing. 'Don't try to continue the ice-maiden act with me. I know you too well, remember? I know the fires that rage beneath that oh, so cool façade.' A tiny smile played about his mouth. 'I also know I'm the only one who can make those fires burn.'

'I hate you, Dane Jacobsen.' She spoke with the venom of thwarted passion, all too painfully aware that he spoke nothing but the truth. No other man could make her body flame as he had done.

'Do you?' His eyebrows quirked sardonically. 'I think you'll find it's not hate that makes you react as you do, Shannon. But perhaps you'll have to grow up a bit more before you realise that.'

He stood up then and walked from the room without so much as a backward glance. Left alone, Shae looked down at her own undone clothing and partly naked body, and shame burned within her. Good lord, she'd all but begged him to take her, yet he'd walked away. She turned her face into the pillow, still trembling with the force of the passion he'd unleased, then left unquenched. Yet, even as anguished sobs racked her body, she could feel no bitterness against him, no trace of the hate she'd claimed. She'd goaded him into doing what he'd done, perhaps even hoping he would take her against her will, she realised in despair. If he had, she could have persuaded herself that none of it had been her fault—that he'd physically forced her into making love.

Marianne's scathing words of earlier played in her mind like a haunting refrain. 'Your sweet, milk-sop charms may be attracting him now,' she'd said, 'but it takes a woman to hold him. A *real* woman.' Shannon had been halfway convinced that he was already sleeping with Marianne, but now she wasn't so sure. The actress had been venomous when she'd chanced upon them in the corridor, but she'd displayed the spitefulness of a disappointed woman, not a wronged one. With her temperament, surely she'd have brought the roof in if she'd discovered her lover in the arms of another woman?

Shannon rolled on to her back, staring through tear-glazed eyes at the ceiling. Perhaps after tonight Marianne would have her desire fulfilled. Perhaps Dane would go unsatisfied from Shae's bed in search of that 'real woman', and he'd find her ready and waiting in Marianne. The voluptuous actress wouldn't need to play foolish games with him.

The thought lit a spark of rebellion, and slowly she sat up, pushing tousled hair back from her tear-streaked face. She'd done nothing but run from Dane from the very start; even now, when she was here in Sheffield with him, she was still running, still afraid of the heartache she must surely face if she allowed the relationship to deepen. Yet what good had running done? Alone in Aberdeen she'd thought about him night and day, had longed with all her heart to be in his arms just once more, had cried herself to sleep night after night only to have her dreams filled with visions of him.

She'd been convinced all along that eventually she must lose him, that Marianne was right—some other attraction must inevitably draw him away. She hadn't changed her mind about that—a man such as Dane would always attract beautiful women, and Shannon could never hope to compete. But would the pain of losing him be any the less simply because she'd managed to hold him at bay? Eventually, probably sooner rather than later, he'd grow tired of waiting for Shannon, and then she'd be left with nothing, in any case. Though she could never let him know it, he already possessed her heart; if she were to give herself to him body and soul, at least the memories would be rich and ultimately fulfilling. Right now all she'd have to look back on would be frustration and longing suppressed by fear.

Reaching a decision, she stood up, groaning as she caught sight of her own rumpled state in the mirror. In this condition she was hardly a siren, she thought with an ironic little smile. But she wasn't a make-up artist for nothing—if she couldn't perform a speedy transformation, then she didn't deserve her job.

Fifteen minutes later she took a deep breath, desperately trying to steady the nerves fluttering like trapped birds in the pit of her stomach. Part of her could barely believe what she was about to do; but the stronger part remained adamant. She might live to rue this impetuous decision, but at least she'd never look back with regret on what might have been if only she'd had the courage to dare.

She checked her reflection, a tiny smile playing about her lips. Even if she said so herself, she was barely recognisable as the young woman who'd been so distraught just a short while ago. Now a poised, elegant creature stared back, dressed in a stylish cowl-necked black dress which swooped dramatically at the back. Knee-length, it showed off her shapely legs in their black stockings and high-heeled shoes in a way that brought a faint flush to her face. It was a dress she'd bought at Kelly's urging, even though she'd been positive she'd never find occasion to wear it.

'Buy it anyway,' Kelly had returned with her usual irresistible persuasiveness. 'It suits you so beautifully it would be a crying shame to let some other woman have it.'

Well, this was hardly the scene she'd have imagined as the perfect time to wear the dress, but now she silently blessed the premonition which had made her pack it along with the predominantly casual clothes she'd chosen to take to Sheffield. She stole a final critical glance at her face, mentally awarding herself top marks for skilful covering of the tear-stains which had marred her skin just a few minutes before. Now her eyes, with their clever shading of amber and gold, shone back at her, large and lustrous—and the lipstick she'd chosen made her mouth look lusciously inviting. She could only hope Dane would feel the same way.

Offering up a quick prayer that she wouldn't bump into any of the other cast members en route, she slipped into the corridor and made her way to Dane's room, pausing at his door to steel herself as another onrush of nerves all but paralysed her. For the first time she wondered what on earth she'd do if Marianne opened the door, and knew with dreadful certainty that she'd never be able to brazen it out. A vision of the other woman's mocking green eyes very nearly sent her running back to the safety of her own room, but having come this far she was determined to see this thing through, come what may.

She lifted her nerveless hand and tapped very quietly on the door, then, gathering up what remained of her courage, knocked more boldly. The door was flung open and she flinched as she found herself staring into Dane's scowling face. His look turned to one of complete amazement as he saw her standing there, a hesitant little smile trembling on her lips.

'Shannon?' He sounded as though he could barely believe the evidence of his own eyes. 'What are you doing here? And why are you dressed like that?'

She made a game effort at a nonchalant shrug.

'We parted on rather poor terms,' she said lightly. 'I've come to—well, to make up. Would you like to offer me a nightcap?'

He stood back to usher her in, his sea-blue eyes still puzzled. 'With pleasure.'

She walked past him into the room, which was very similar to her own in style, but which bore the unmistakably masculine stamp of its occupant. He must have been about to take a shower, she realised, noticing a towel flung carelessly on to the bed, and seeing for the first time that his shirt was undone almost to the waist, revealing his broad, muscular chest with its lavish covering of silky golden hair. The sight made her swallow convulsively, and unconsciously she curled her fingers into the palms of her hands to stop herself from simply reaching out to touch his skin.

'What's this all about, Shae?' he said gravely.

'You said. . .' The words blocked in her throat as her eyes begged him to help her out.

'I said?'

She took a deep breath and tried again.

'You said you'd wait for me to come to you.' Now the words tumbled out in a rush. 'Here I am.'

He walked over to her then and placed his hands on her shoulders. She trembled beneath his touch, feeling the warmth of his fingers even through the material of her dress. For a long, endless moment he gazed into her eyes as though searching for answers, then he released her.

'I think we both need a drink,' he said gruffly. 'What will you have?'

She let out the breath she hadn't even realised she'd been holding.

'A whisky, please, if you have one.'

He crossed the room to the drinks cabinet, and poured two healthy measures of Scotch, adding a splash of soda before handing one to Shannon. Her fingers were shaking so much that she was forced to lay the glass on a nearby table after taking a sip of the warming amber liquid.

'Sit down.'

She perched herself uncomfortably on the only chair in the room as he sat down on the bed. This was proving even harder than she'd anticipated, she thought, nervous hilarity bubbling up inside her. She'd come to seduce the man, for goodness' sake; right now she felt more like an job applicant attending an important interview.

'Why now, Shae?'

She reached for the glass, delaying the moment when she'd have to answer, unsure even how to answer.

'Is it because of what happened this evening?' His eyes bored into her, their expression unreadable.

'That's partly it, I suppose.' She found it hard to talk objectively about such an emotive subject. She hadn't really imagined she'd have to talk at all, she realised—had hoped and assumed he'd simply sweep her into his arms. She should have known to expect the unexpected where he was concerned. 'But I also decided I was tired of running from you.'

He nodded thoughtfully, his eyes never leaving her face. 'Why *have* you been running from me, Shae?'

The question made her flinch, and she took another quick sip of whisky.

'Come to that,' he went on inexorably, 'why have you spent your whole life running?'

Her eyes widened. 'What makes you think I have?' she parried.

He shrugged. 'You said yourself it's not common to find a twenty-seven-year-old virgin in these so-called permissive times.' He fingered his chin consideringly. 'Since you're a very beautiful woman; we can immediately rule out the possibility that that no one's ever been sufficiently attracted to you that they would attempt to storm your female bastions—which leaves another couple of options. One is that you're frigid. . .' He paused, smiling slightly. 'We both know that's not the case. The other is that for some reason you've been too scared to let anyone close enough.'

'It could be that I've simply never felt strongly enough about anyone,' she cut in, instantly wishing the words unsaid as she realised how much they revealed about her feelings for him.

He nodded, appearing not to notice the blush staining her cheeks.

'That's also true, of course, but I don't believe you've ever allowed yourself to try. You're afraid to trust—you've erected barriers against the world, Shannon Lea. I was aware of that the very first time I met you.' He paused to refill his glass, then held the whisky bottle out to her, but she shook her head. If ever she needed a clear head, it was now.

'Why are you putting me through this, Dane?' She was aware of the tremor in her voice. 'Why can't you simply. . .?'

'Take you to bed?' The ghost of a smile glimerered

in his eyes. 'You still believe that's all I want from you?'

'Isn't it?' She gazed at him in confusion. Would she ever understand this complex man?

'No, dammit, and it never has been.' A muscle twitched in his cheek, and for the first time she was aware of his tension. But why should he be tense? She was here for the taking, wasn't she? He got to his feet and paced restlessly about the room, then crouched down before her chair.

'I want more than your body,' he said quietly, 'though lord knows it's given me a few sleepless nights! But I won't make love to you while your mind's still closed to me, Shannon Lea.' He took her hand in his, gently playing with her fingers. 'You have to let those barriers fall, Shae. Trust me.'

She hung her head, feeling tears prickle in her eyes. Things weren't turning out as she'd expected at all; now she was dazed, confused, hardly knew where she was or what she was saying.

'It's hard,' she said at last, her words barely audible.

'I know that.' The blue eyes were sympathetic, yet implacable. 'The best things in life often are hard. But I won't accept half-measures. Will you trust me, Shannon? Will you open up to me and tell me what it is that's made you hide your heart away for so long?'

For a long moment there was silence between them as she stared unseeingly down at her own hand caught in his surprisingly tender grasp. She felt as though she were standing on the edge of a great chasm, with him on the other side urging her to jump across to him. The choice—and the danger—was clear. Making that choice could rip her in two. At last she gave a barely perceptible nod, and he stood up, gently tugging her to her feet.

'Come on,' he said quietly. 'Come sit beside me on the bed.'

For a fleeting second as she crossed the floor Shannon was all but swamped by a feeling of panic that bade her run now, while she still had the chance. But when Dane sat down and pulled her against him, wrapping his arms warmly about her, she knew the time for running was over. Whatever the outcome, whatever his reaction, he had to know the truth.

She took a deep, unsteady breath, her voice low and uncertain, sounding alien to her own ears as she began her story.

'It all began before I was born,' she said, unaware that she was twisting her hands tightly together in her lap. 'My mother was an innocent young country lass, born and brought up in a tiny village in the far north of Scotland. By rights she should have remained there all her life, marrying one of the village lads, or a local farmer, and raising a parcel of kids, just as her mother and grandmother and goodness knows how many other generations had done before her.' She smiled wryly. 'The pace of life is slow there—things take a long time in changing. Anyway, one day a young man came into the shop where she worked. He was very good-looking, very charming, and had a kind of city slickness she'd never encountered before. She was fascinated when he said he came from London—as far as she was concerned he might as well have come from the Moon, because she had as little likelihood of ever visiting either.'

She paused, imagining the scene in her mind's eye as she had done so many times before, trying to picture her mother as a young girl, still in the fresh-faced bloom of youth. 'He told her his name was William, and that he was working in the north for a little while. My mother was so dazzled she never even thought to question him about his job, but she grew to live for the visits he made daily to the shop. Eventually he asked her out, and, even though she knew her parents strongly disapproved of the flashy young man from London, she disobeyed them and started sneaking out of the house every night when they were asleep, to meet him.

'After a few weeks he told her he was going home, and asked her to go with him. By that time he'd turned her head so much with tales of the big city and the life they could have there, she'd have followed him anywhere. That night she sneaked out of the house as usual, but this time she was carrying a case. William met her as they'd arranged, and they quietly disappeared, like two thieves in the night.'

'Did he take her to London?' Dane softly prompted her as she lapsed into a musing silence. She nodded, a frown darkening her features.

'He took her all right—took her to the kind of life she could never have dreamed of. William was a gambler, ready to try his luck at anything. Horses, cards, roulette—he didn't care what the game was. When he was winning, they lived in style. But he didn't often win.' She stared ahead, unseeingly. 'Gambling became an obsession with him, eventually he lost everything they possessed, and my mother begged and pleaded with him to give it all up—to find an ordinary job and give up the gaming life. He promised he would—after he'd had one last crack at success.'

Dane's arms tightened about her, as though he

could feel the pain she was suffering, and she took a deep, unsteady breath.

'A big poker-game was being planned. William had no stake. He tried, with three other men, to rob a bank. It was a failure. William was shot dead.' The agony of years was held in those short staccato sentences, and tears glimmered in her tawny eyes with the pain of confession.

'Go on,' Dane said quietly.

'Are you sure?' She tried to pull away from his comforting arms, but he held fast. 'Haven't I shocked you enough? Haven't I outraged your sensibilities sufficiently yet?'

He smiled faintly. 'My sensibilities can stand a lot of outrage,' he returned. 'Go on with the story.'

'If only it were just a story.' Her eyes reflected her anguish. 'But it isn't. It's the real-life tale of a foolish young woman who fell in love with a handsome, no-good man, and had her life ruined because of it. William, as you'll doubtless have gathered by now, was my father. Unfortunately,' she went on, her voice heavy with sarcasm, 'he never actually got round to marrying my mother so, on top of everything else, she had to cope with the stigma of an illegitimate child.'

'What did she do?'

'Do?' She twisted her head to look at him through strangely unfocused eyes. 'She did the only thing she could under the circumstances. She went home to the loving, welcoming arms of her own family.'

'Did they welcome her?'

Shannon gave a bleak little laugh. 'What do you think? Don't forget, she was returning to a village in the north, hardly the most progressive or liberal-minded place at the best of times, and this particular village was especially proud of its moral record. Other places might have the shame of illicit love affairs and babies born out of wedlock, but not theirs.

'On top of that, my grandfather was a particularly stalwart member of the church—one who'd always been admired, feared even, for his rigid adherence to the faith.' Unconsciously she laced her fingers together. 'To have his daughter run away from home in the first place had been a bitter blow. To have her return complete with illegitimate child nearly felled him completely.'

'"Suffer little children to come unto Me,"' Dane quoted softly. 'It doesn't say anywhere in the Bible that only those with married parents will be accepted.'

Shannon pursed her lips. 'My grandfather could probably have taken you unerringly to the chapter and verse which said exactly that,' she averred. 'As far as he was concerned, God created sex purely for the purposes of procreation. Anyone who indulged in it for its own sake was an out-and-out sinner—and that went for the resulting offspring, too.'

'The sins of the father,' Dane murmured, gently twisting a lock of her hair in his fingers. 'Did he expect you to turn out like William?'

'Expect it?' She gave a dry little laugh. 'He said it was inevitable, that bad blood would always surface in the next generation, and that the only way he could hope to save me was to chase the devil from my soul before he got a proper hold.'

'Chase the devil?' Dane's eyebrows drew together thunderously. 'He didn't ever hit you, did he?'

Shae shook her head. 'No. He wasn't a bad man, Dane—he simply lived life according to very strict rules.' Her eyes clouded over with the pain of the memories being allowed to surface after so many years of being ruthlessly suppressed. 'He's dead now, but my mother still lives in the village. She never married. She's always been a rather unhappy, bitter woman.'

Dane narrowed his eyes, clearly understanding the depths of anguish that lay behind the stark summary of one woman's life.

'How did you find out about your father, Shae?'

'How do you think?' She gave the ghost of a smile. 'In the primary-school playground, of course, when I was singled out to stand in the centre of a ring while a dozen sweet-faced little girls danced round me chanting "Shannon's dad's a robber."' She shuddered at the memory, and Dane's lips tightened to a narrow white line.

'What did you do?'

'Do? I picked a fight with the biggest one, which turned into a full-pitch playground battle, and went home with a bloody nose, two black eyes and a front tooth missing.' Her sherry-coloured eyes danced with mischievous amusement. 'To my eternal pride, the others all looked worse!'

'What did your grandfather say?'

The laughter fled from her eyes as quickly as it had come. 'He told me I had no right to inflict pain on those girls, because they'd simply been telling the truth.'

'Good lord, Shae, the man was inhuman!' The words burst from him in an angry rush, and she glanced at him in surprise. 'How could he possibly let a little innocent girl be bullied and tormented?'

For a terrible moment Shannon thought she would give way to tears, and knew it was because of his fury on her behalf. At best she had expected bland sympathy from him, but the sparks shooting in his eyes were genuine. For so long she'd held the secrets of her past under lock and key, barely allowing even Kelly much more than a glimpse into her background. Now, for reasons she still couldn't fully fathom, she was lifting curtains to reveal all to a man who was, in truth, little more than a stranger—and he was reacting as if he were a long-lost brother. Or a lover.

That errant thought, coming from goodness knew where, made her heart beat an erratic tattoo. For heaven's sake, Shae, she told herself desperately, he's being nice to you, but don't lose your head over it. He's an actor, he can be anything he wants, to anybody, just as the occasion warrants. This is just an excellent piece of acting, that's all.

Even as she silently repeated the words she found herself looking into his sea-deep eyes, wishing she could drown in them. This man would look after you. He'd keep you safe. Her eyes flew wide open, the voice in her mind so clear that she felt sure he must have heard it too.

'Are you all right, Shae?'

'What? I'm sorry, Dane, I was miles away.' She blinked, desperately trying to shake her thoughts back to some sort of rationality.

'There's one thing I still don't understand,' he said musingly.

'Just one?' As smiles went it was a poor effort, but all she could manage under the circumstances.

'Just one for now.' The understanding in his eyes reached out to her, warming the frozen places in her soul. 'What was William doing in the village in the first place? He was obviously a city kid through and through.'

A sad little smile curved her lips. 'I think, for perhaps the first and only time in his life, William had been trying to shake off his obsession, and he did it by getting as far away from temptation as possible. It didn't work. The lure of gambling ultimately proved too much for him.'

Dane shook his head wonderingly. 'I don't know how you've managed to carry all of this around with you for so long and still be a relatively sane, level-headed person.'

'That's not what you thought of me when I tried to run from you in Glenshee.' In a bid to lighten the atmosphere she was quite willing to poke fun at herself.

His features remained serious. 'I understand now that you were trying to run from a situation you thought you couldn't handle. Now I've heard about your past, I can't even blame you.' He leaned closer, his blue eyes compelling. 'But Shannon, you have it in you to fight the ghosts—to face up to them and banish them forever. None of the things that happened before you were born were your fault; they weren't really anyone's fault, if it comes to that—simply the capricious workings of fate. You don't have to carry that with you like a millstone for the rest of your life. Lay it down now.'

She leaned back against him, revelling in the strength and warmth of his body, allowing herself for a few luxurious moments the unaccustomed joy of feeling secure in his embrace.

'Can I stay with you tonight, Dane?' she murmured softly. He kissed her hair.

'Do you think I'd let you go now?' Gently he turned her in his arms to face him, and he kissed her very tenderly on the lips. 'Let's go to bed. I want to hold you properly.'

'Do you mind if I take a shower first?' She felt strangely shy about undressing in front of him, and the look in his eyes told her he understood.

'Go ahead. I'll be waiting.'

In the bathroom she slipped out of her clothes and stepped under the jet of warm water, letting it ease away some of the strain. When she returned to the bedroom, clad only in a towel, he was already in bed, and he smiled softly.

'Come on, little one.'

She slid under the quilt and into his welcoming arms with a small sigh. Even though she knew in her heart of hearts that this could never last, she felt as though she'd reached a safe harbour after sailing in a vast, unfriendly sea.

CHAPTER EIGHT

SHANNON awoke the following morning still wrapped in Dane's arms, and contentment washed over her in a warm wave. For perhaps the first time in her life there was no feeling of restlessness deep in her soul, no desire to be somewhere else. Telling Dane about her past had removed a massive weight from her shoulders, she realised with a sense of wonder and gratitude. It had been a sweet night—the shadows growing deeper as they'd talked, until she'd finally drifted off to sleep with his arms tight about her and his lips on her hair. Now, with the faint light of morning appearing through the curtains, she was content simply to gaze on his sleeping features, wishing the moment would never end, wishing she could lie here forever, holding the man who held her heart.

Impulsively she touched her lips to his shoulder and he stirred sleepily, smiling as he opened his eyes.

'Good morning, little one,' he said softly. 'Did you sleep well?'

She nodded, unable for the moment to speak.

'You look beautiful.'

'Beautiful?' She laughed happily, remembering the pains she'd gone to the previous evening. 'But my hair's a mess and I. . .'

'You're beautiful to me.' He kissed her lightly, and the touch of his lips sent an exquisite shiver through her entire body. She slid her arms round his neck and he groaned softly, deep in his throat, his hands moving downwards to caress her silky skin. His kiss deepened, and unconsciously she arched up towards him, aching for his touch.

The moment was shattered as the telephone on the bedside-table suddenly discovered its voice, and Dane cursed quietly under his breath.

'It's my alarm call,' he said frustratedly. 'Ignore it.'

Shannon shook her head with a regretful smile. 'You know we can't. This is dress rehearsal day, remember? And I have to meet with Josh first thing.'

He slid one hand down to cup her naked breast, and the breath blocked in her throat as his thumb teased one nipple.

'Then I suggest we reconvene our own meeting at the earliest possible opportunity. Do you agree, Miss Lea?'

The look in his eyes would have made her agree to anything, she thought dazedly, only just managing to summon up enough co-ordination to nod her head.

'Whatever you say, Mr Jacobsen,' she murmured huskily, and he pulled her to him for a last long kiss that left her breathless and trembling.

'Now go, woman, before I padlock the door and hold you prisoner here for the rest of the day, as my sensible ancestors would have done!' He gave her a gentle push, and she slid from beneath the covers, blushing faintly as his eyes swept boldly over her nakedness, yet enjoying his frank scrutiny at the same time. Marianne might dismiss her 'milk-sop charms' with contempt, but for the moment, at least, Dane felt rather differently, and the knowledge made her blood sing.

* * *

The morning passed by in a flurry of activity, and she barely saw Dane, except for a fleeting moment as he rushed headlong along the corridor, pausing long enough to drop a kiss on her lips that turned her knees to water. Later, she made her way up to the stage wings, driven by a sheer need to see him. He was in the middle of the pivotal scene with Marianne, a scene which called on hero and heroine to embrace and kiss passionately.

It was clear that the actress was intent on enjoying this part of the play to the full, Shae thought wryly, resolutely quashing the niggling little stab of jealousy as Dane took her in his arms. Marianne's hands snaked up behind his neck, her fingers losing themselves in his thick golden hair as she pulled his face down to her own. The kiss seemed to last forever, but as they finally pulled apart Marianne shot a triumphant glance over Dane's shoulder into the wings.

'Don't let her get to you,' a voice murmured at her side, and she looked up to see one of the other actors, a tall good-looking young man called Gavin James. 'She's making a meal of it quite deliberately because she knows you're standing here.'

'Really?'

'Sure.' He grinned boyishly, displaying a mouthful of beautifully capped white teeth. 'Marianne likes being Queen Bee in the hive. You've pushed her nose out of joint.' He glanced back towards the stage. 'If you stay here she'll probably call for a dozen more rehearsals of that damn kiss—so why don't we cut out of here for a while and go for a coffee? I'm not needed just now.'

'I really shouldn't,' Shae began, but he took her arm firmly.

'Come on. Don't give her the satisfaction of knowing you're watching.'

In the theatre coffee-bar he brought them both a drink, then settled himself comfortably opposite her.

'This is the first time I've had a chance to talk to you on your own,' he said thoughtfully, a speculative gleam in his hazel eyes. 'How long have you known Dane?'

'A while,' she said, made faintly uncomfortable by his directness.

'You've worked together before?'

'Yes.'

'Aha.' Gavin leaned over the table and gently tipped her chin upwards so that she was forced to look into his eyes. 'I thought as much. There's been a lot of conjecture about the two of you, you know.'

'I really don't see why.'

He grinned. 'Perhaps it's got something to do with the way Dane looks at you when you're not aware of it—or vice versa. Or the way Marianne practically goes up in smoke when she sees you together.' He lounged back in his seat, thoroughly enjoying himself. 'I am right, aren't I? You two are "an item", as they used to say in Noel Coward's days?'

'Gavin, I barely know you, yet you're asking questions about my personal life.' She tried to look annoyed, but the teasing warmth in his hazel eyes disarmed her, and she found herself laughing along with him.

'I fear, Miss Lea, you'll find there's no such thing as a "personal life" in the theatre, and certainly not a private one. We're a pretty gossipy lot, if truth be told.' He wagged a playfully warning finger in her direction. 'So if you possess any skeletons in your cupboard, I suggest you lock them in very tightly indeed, otherwise they'll all come tumbling out.'

The smile froze on her face as his words, jocular though they were meant to be, slammed home with the force of a bullet. It had been hard enough telling Dane about her past, but the thought of her background becoming common knowledge was horrifying.

'Hey, have I touched a raw nerve?' Gavin looked faintly concerned. 'I'm sorry, Shannon, I didn't mean. . .'

'Is this a private party or can anyone join in?'

Her thoughts still whirling, Shae looked up to see Marianne standing by the table, her green eyes calculating and faintly malicious as she glanced from Shannon to Gavin. Abruptly Shae stood up.

'I have to go. I have work to do.'

'Don't go on my account.' Marianne raised her eyebrows archly.

'I'm not. But I really must go.' Shae turned and all but ran from the coffee-bar, ignoring Gavin when he called after her. In the make-up room she collapsed into a chair, dropping her head into her hands and groaning heavily. Despite what Dane had said about facing up to the ghosts in her past and laying them to rest, it seemed she was still to be haunted by them. It had never counted for anything that she'd been the innocent victim, that she'd had no control over the events which had shaped her life—she'd carried the burden with her, locked into her soul, and at least that way she'd felt relatively safe. Last night she'd lifted the barriers to allow Dane in. Had it been the biggest mistake of her life?

Gavin had said the theatre crowd were a gossipy lot—what if Dane found her story too good to keep to himself? The very prospect of her life being picked over like some succulent titbit chilled her to the bone.

Moving on automatic pilot, she forced herself to tidy up the make-up room, washing sponges and organising the cosmetics she'd need the following evening when the play had its first-night performance. She was still there some time later when Dane entered the room, a faint weariness evident in his vivid blue eyes.

'The director's finally decided to call it a day,' he said.

'Was the rehearsal a success?' she asked stiltedly, still plagued by the doubts that had been besetting her ever since leaving Gavin.

'Heaven forbid,' he smiled. 'You know theatre superstition, Shae—a good dress rehearsal means a lousy first night. However, we managed between us to make sure things didn't go according to plan—or to script.' He sat down with a sigh, rubbing one hand over his eyes. 'In fact I've got to have one last brainstorming session with the director before I leave.' He glanced up, and the warmth in his expression sent a tremor through her chilled soul. 'Come here,' he commanded softly.

For a moment she wanted to rebel, to pull back from the brink even at this stage of the game. But she couldn't do it, couldn't turn away from him now when she so desperately needed the reassuring warmth and strength of his embrace. With a tiny sigh she crossed the room towards him and he drew her on to his lap, his arms tight about her.

'Lord, you feel good,' he murmured into her hair. 'And you smell so sweet, like wild flowers in a meadow. I wish I could just spirit you back to my bed right now and spend hours making love to you.' He stroked a stray curl back from her cheek. 'I want to hold you in my arms and kiss you till we're both half crazy with it.'

Shae leaned against him, dizzied by the mental pictures he was creating, and when he kissed her the touch of his lips sent a scorching heat right through her.

Suddenly she felt a glowing warmth deep inside; he could never betray her, could never sell what they had together for the cheap thrill of recounting an old, sordid story. Her secrets were safe in his keeping.

They sat together for a few moments more, then he groaned.

'I have to go, Shae. The director's waiting for me now.' He kissed her tenderly. 'Why don't you go back to the hotel, relax for a while? Tonight we can go out for a quiet meal together, and then. . .' His eyes gleamed, and she laughed.

'And then we can each have an early night,' she said mischievously. 'After all, we didn't get much sleep last night.'

He stood up, setting her carefully on her feet, then swatted her playfully on the backside.

'Wretch,' he smiled. 'If you're tired, Miss Lea, I suggest you catch up on some sleep when you go back to the hotel. Because you sure won't be getting much of it later tonight.'

She was still smiling at his words a couple of hours later, back in her room. She had tried to catch a quick nap, but anticipation of the evening to come had fluttered within her like a hummingbird, refusing to let her settle. Instead, she took a long, hot bath, scattering in a lavish handful of scented flakes and letting the perfumed water ease some of the tension from her body. She'd over-reacted to Gavin's teasing. Dane was the only one here who knew of her background. He wouldn't let her down. She'd stake her life—and her love for him—on that.

She lay back in the water, closing her eyes as the water lapped softly against her skin. Tonight she would make love for the first time—and it would be with the man she loved. She was under no illusions—she knew he could never feel the same way about her, she knew too that she was storing up heartbreak for herself. But right now it didn't matter. Right now she would grab what life was offering with both hands.

'"Better to have loved and lost",' she quoted softly to herself, then a smile of sheer female pleasure curved her lips as she heard the sounds of tapping on her bedroom door. They'd arranged to meet for dinner, but it seemed he hadn't been able to wait. He'd come straight to her after leaving the theatre, and his impatience thrilled her to the core.

She climbed from the water and wrapped a towel about her wet body, padding barefoot across the carpet, a soft light of welcome playing in her eyes as she opened the door. The light died instantly as she found herself looking not at Dane, but at Marianne.

'Can I help you?' she said evenly, unconsciously pulling the towel a little more tightly about her.

'That depends,' Marianne purred silkily, and Shae was hard pressed not to shudder at the malicious pleasure in the other woman's green eyes. 'I want to talk to you.'

'As you can see, I've just come out of the bath,' Shae said, striving to remain polite, when every instinct in her soul was screaming at her to send the actress running with her tail between her legs. 'This really isn't a good time.'

'I think you'll find it's as good a time as any.' Marianne tossed her head, sending her glorious hair rippling in turbulent waves over her shoulders.

'Very well. Come in.'

Marianne crossed the room with her usual catlike grace and threw herself casually down on the bed. Feeling strangely vulnerable in her near-naked state, Shae picked up a dressing-gown and shrugged her shoulders into it.

'Now. What did you want to see me about?'

'Simply to tell you that I've been having a most interesting conversation.' Marianne's eyes gleamed malevolently. 'My dear Shannon, for someone so pitifully characterless, you really have had the most fascinating life.'

Shae flinched violently. 'What do you mean by that?' The tremor in her voice was clear even to her own ears.

Marianne stretched languorously, lifting her mane of hair from her neck. 'Come, Shannon, let's not play games. I think you know exactly what I mean.'

Inwardly praying this was all nothing more than a clever bluff, Shannon stood her ground.

'Explain it to me.'

'Do you really want me to go into all the nasty, seedy little details? I'd have assumed you'd know them well enough without wishing to hear them repeated.' Her eyes narrowed viciously. 'Tell me, just what is it like growing up knowing you're the bastard offspring of a criminal? And what's it like knowing your dear daddy died in a shoot-out? Did he manage to take anyone else out before he died, Shannon? Was he a murderer as well as a common thug?'

Shannon started to shake, hearing again the playground taunts, seeing the looks in the eyes of the children as they danced about her, holding hands and chanting, keeping her captive in the middle of the circle.

'How did you find out?' she whispered.

'How do you think?' The venomous triumph in Marianne's voice cut like a whiplash.

'Dane.' Her knees threatened to give way beneath her.

Marianne shrugged negligently. 'Did you really think you could keep it to yourself? You're a fool.'

A greater fool than you could ever know, Shae thought dully, pain throbbing like a drum beat at her temples. She'd given him her trust and he'd thrown it back in her face, practically falling over himself in his haste to share the story with this woman.

'Does everyone know?' she asked quietly.

'They soon will.' Marianne laughed delightedly. 'Just think, Shae, perhaps Josh could use your story. What a tale of human degradation—it would make a marvellous play!' She got to her feet, carefully brushing a non-existent piece of lint from her skin-tight leggings. 'I think I'll suggest it to him. I could even play the lead role.' She threw a withering glance in Shae's direction. 'So long as he promised to give the heroine more character and personality, that is. I doubt I could manage to play anyone as colourless as you.'

For an agonising moment Shannon felt herself losing control, overwhelmed by an urge to fly at Marianne, to assuage her own brutal torment by lashing out as she had done long ago in the school playground, when the jeers and mockery became too much to bear. But, as her grandfather had drummed into her then, she had no right to inflict pain simply because the other person was telling a truth that was hard for her to cope with. As Marianne walked to the door, she turned away, unable to look at the woman who'd brought her world crashing about her ears like a fragile house of cards.

'Something tells me you won't be joining us for dinner tonight.' Marianne laughed as she twisted the knife still deeper. 'I don't suppose anyone will even notice you're not there. And don't worry about Dane—I'll look after him.'

The door closed behind her, and Shannon sank to her knees on the floor, unable to bear the weight of the pain any longer.

CHAPTER NINE

SHANNON never knew how long she lay slumped on the floor, racked by the agony of Dane's betrayal, immobilised by sheer unremitting pain, yet unable even to find relief in tears. Only the realisation that he would soon be arriving at her door finally roused her from her misery, spurred her into action. She had to get away—had to put as much distance as she possibly could between herself and the man who'd abused her trust so callously.

A tiny part of her wanted to confront him with what he'd done; yet she knew she couldn't do it, couldn't bear looking into his sea-blue eyes, or at the lips which had kissed her so tenderly the night before, only to laugh with Marianne today as he shared with her the secrets Shannon had confided so trustingly—so blindly! For one desperate moment she allowed herself to question whether he really had done it, but knew there could be no other answer. Dane was the only person here who knew of her past. The story couldn't possibly have been passed on by anyone else.

Moving like an automaton, she dressed in jeans and a warm sweater, smiling mirthlessly as she realised this was the third time she'd been forced to flee from Dane Jacobsen. Well, flight hadn't worked on the other two occasions, but, for the sake of her own sanity, this had to be third time lucky. Picking up her jacket, she closed her eyes. If only she'd never met him—had never experienced the exquisite sweetness of being held against his heart—she wouldn't now be crushed under the weight of this unbearable sorrow.

She slipped quietly out of the hotel, grateful that none of the other cast members were around to witness her departure, and made her way to the car park. As she climbed into the driver's seat of her own car, she realised she had no plan in mind, no destination. She didn't know a single soul outwith the theatre company in this part of the world. Josh Thayer's warm brown eyes swam before her, and for a moment she wished she could simply find him and throw herself into his comforting arms. Then she remembered Marianne, and her taunts that Shae's story would make a terrific play, and gave a hopeless shrug. Much as she'd liked Josh, she couldn't be sure Marianne wasn't right—and if Dane could let her down, then why shouldn't his playwright friend?

Driving away into the city streets, she'd never felt so alone or so friendless in her entire life. Kelly would understand, of course, but she was many miles away, working on location, and Shae didn't even have a contact number. Well, she'd spent most of her life flying solo, protecting herself from the rest of the world behind high barriers; now, after risking and losing all in one fell swoop, she'd simply have to set about the painful business of re-erecting those walls.

She drove aimlessly for hours, stopping to fill the car with petrol, then carrying on, barely noticing where she was going. Dane and Marianne would probably be together right now back at the hotel, and she wondered just how he would be feeling. Would he suffer even a second's remorse? It seemed unlikely—perhaps he'd even be grateful to Marianne, for getting Shae out of his life.

Finally, worn out by her own thoughts and the strain of thc last few hours, she drew up at a small country hotel and took a room there for the night.

Behind the closed door of her bedroom, she pulled off her boots, threw her jacket on to a chair, and collapsed on to the single bed. Unthinkingly she glanced at the clock on the bedside-table and tears stung her eyes. This time last night she'd been lying in Dane's arms, feeling safe, secure, at peace with the world for perhaps the first time in her troubled life. How could she have been such a fool? Angrily she dashed the tears away with the back of one hand, refusing to give in to weakness and self-pity. Now she needed all the strength she could muster if she was to start putting her life back together.

She hadn't expected to get much sleep, but exhaustion finally overcame her and she lapsed into a fitful, restless doze, tossing and turning through the long night as dreams haunted her mind. She awoke to a cold, grey morning, feeling stiff and uncomfortable, and uttered a hollow groan as she realised she'd fallen asleep in her clothes. Now, on top of everything else, she looked like something the cat had dragged in, and she hadn't even brought a change of clothes with her, having planned to return to the Sheffield hotel to collect her luggage and settle her bill at a time when the actors would be at the theatre.

She gazed dispiritedly into the mirror, and the face looking back was like that of a stranger, pale and hollow-eyed. She attempted to restore some order to her tousled hair with her fingers, then stroked on a little blusher to counteract at least a little of her pallor; but there was little she could do to repair the ravages of the night, and finally she turned away with a heavy sigh.

She ate a solitary breakfast in the hotel dining-room, turning down the waitress's offer of bacon and eggs with as much grace as she could muster, feeling faintly sick at the thought of food. Instead she sipped on several cups of reviving, strong black coffee, and chewed listlessly on a piece of cardboard masquerading as toast.

After settling her bill, she went for a walk through the hotel grounds, ending up beside a pretty little river meandering gently through a meadow, and sat down on a boulder, barely feeling the coolness of the air as she gazed into the silvery, rippling waters. She stayed there for some time, the heavy depression that had been weighing her down ever since Marianne had appeared in her room soothed a little by the gentle singing of the river.

Suddenly she sat bolt upright, horrified as a new thought struck home. Incredible as it seemed, she'd been too caught up in her own unhappiness to give a second's thought to the play, which was due to open that very evening. There was no way the actors and actresses could possibly manage the complicated looks she'd created cosmetically, by themselves. They might be able to contrive something, but Josh had been adamant that the highly distinctive, futuristic styles were essential to the whole atmosphere and setting of the drama.

She dropped her head into her hands with a despairing groan. She couldn't go back and face them all—not now, not when Marianne would have told them all about her criminal father, doubtless revelling in every sad little detail, probably creating a few more just to spice the story up still more. Most of all she couldn't face Dane, couldn't cope with the new pain that seeing him again must surely bring. But she couldn't just desert them, either; for several members of the cast this play of Josh Thayer's was the first decent break they'd had, and she knew from dressing-room conversations just how much personal and emotional investment they'd made in its succcess. They could perhaps find a replacement make-up artist, though that would prove difficult at such short notice, but someone coming in at the last moment would find it hard to cope with the unusual styles, and the actors would be having problems enough dealing with first-night nerves without having to face any added strain.

Turmoil raged within her as she battled to find an answer to the seemingly insurmountable dilemma, and she raised her eyes to the grey skies as though a solution could be found there. But at last she got to her feet, drawing herself up to her full height, trying somehow to muster strength for what she had to face. In truth, there was no choice; no matter what the cost to herself, she couldn't let Josh and the others down. She had to go back to the theatre and see this thing through, for tonight, at least.

And there was more. Dane had told her she had to stop running from the ghosts in her past, and suddenly she realised that in that, at least, he was right. She had to turn and fight, to face her accusers with her head held high and her dignity intact. To flee would be to award them victory—and, for the first time, she knew a burning determination to win. She could never hope to rescue her heart, but at least she could salvage her pride.

* * *

The first person she met when she walked through the backstage door was Josh, and, if the situation hadn't been so terrible, his expression—which somehow managed to combine outrage, amazement and sheer blessed relief—would have been positively comical. As she walked uncertainly towards him, he gave a great bellow, then flung his arms about her, all but suffocating her in his bear-like embrace.

'Where the hell have you been, woman?'

'I'm sorry, Josh. I know it was irresponsible and unforgivable of me to disappear on opening night.'

'Never mind that! I've been going half crazy with worry wondering what on earth had happened to you.' He held her away to arm's length, his kindly brown eyes sweeping her face as though searching for clues. 'What happened, Shae?' he said quietly.

The warmth in his voice reached out to her, thawing the numb, frozen parts deep inside, and she choked back a sob. She'd anticipated anger and scorn on her return to the theatre, and Josh's totally unexpected concern all but unmanned her.

'Don't you know?' she whispered.

He shook his head.

'I thought you must have had an accident—I even checked out the hospitals this morning.' His eyes narrowed. 'Good lord, girl, you look terrible. Has someone done something to upset you?'

She closed her eyes briefly. She'd been so sure that Marianne would waste no time in spreading her poison—now she didn't know how to start explaining her disappearance.

'It's a long story, Josh,' she said at last. 'I will tell you, but not now.'

'You don't have to tell me a thing,' he said firmly,

and she felt a rush of grateful affection. 'I'm just glad to have you back safe and sound.' He gave a wry little chuckle. 'Now all we need is to find Dane, and we've got a show!'

'Find Dane?' His words took her completely by surprise. 'Why, what's happened to him?'

'When he discovered you'd disappeared, he went storming off half cocked and in a filthy rage that would have rocked the very mountains. I haven't seen him since this morning.'

Shannon laid a hand on his arm, her expression drawn and worried.

'I'm so sorry, Josh, this is all my fault.'

Despite all, he was able to grin, his white teeth gleaming through the shaggy beard.

'Don't worry, Shae, I'm sure he'll return to the fold too. In any case, young Gavin can always fill his shoes if he doesn't appear—he's been acting as understudy. I was a lot more worried about you—versatile I might be, but I'd never have been able to do the make-up you've created!'

Since it was Dane's name on the hoardings which had sold out the theatre on opening night and for several weeks to come, Josh's kindness brought a painful lump to her throat, and she could only gaze at him in mute gratitude.

'Now come on,' he said gruffly, 'let's get you started on the rest of the cast. You've got a lot of greasepaint to get through before they're ready to hit the stage.'

He walked along the corridor with her, giving her shoulder a comforting squeeze as they parted at the make-up room door.

'I'd better go and reassure the director that you're

back. He was just about to start on his nineteenth nervous breakdown when I left him.'

She watched him stroll away down the corridor as if he hadn't a care in the world, knowing full well he was putting the act on for her benefit, and that he must be worrying about the star performer who was also his best friend. But where on earth could Dane be? She frowned in puzzlement—it just didn't make sense. Why should he disappear?

She walked into the make-up room, then stopped in her tracks at the sight of Marianne sitting in the chair before the mirror.

'Well, well, well.' The actress swivelled round to face her in the doorway. 'If it isn't the prodigal daughter. What happened, Shannon? Couldn't you find a bank to rob or a car to steal?'

Loathing for the other woman rose in Shae's chest like an icy-cold wave, but she resolutely contained the feeling, staring back at her with a bland expression that gave nothing of her inner turmoil away. After a moment she walked across the room and placed her hands on the two arms of the chair, effectively pinning Marianne in place.

'Listen to me,' she said quietly. 'I came back because I didn't want to let Josh and the others down. I want to see them all do the best they can, because they deserve it. As for you, I couldn't care less if you walked out on to that stage with a sack over your head.'

Marianne's green eyes flew wide open.

'How dare you talk to me like that, you little guttersnipe?' she spat. 'I'll make sure you never work in theatre again after this.'

Shae shrugged. 'I no longer care what you do to

me. Now, do you want me to do your make-up, or not? The choice is yours.'

Suppressed fury sparked flames in the woman's catlike eyes, and for a second Shae thought she would storm out of the room. It was clear she was waging an internal battle with herself, but finally the actress in her won out, and she tossed her luxuriant hair back contemptuously.

'You might as well,' she said disdainfully. 'It's all you're good for, after all. Perhaps Dane will finally realise that for himself now.'

Shae worked swiftly, reluctant to be in the woman's company for a split second longer than was absolutely necessary. Still, when she stepped back to survey her own handiwork, she allowed herself a moment of professional pride. Dislike might be bubbling inside her like bitter acid, but it hadn't prevented her from doing a good job.

Marianne took a cursory glance at her own reflection and pursed her lips disgustedly.

'Is this the best you can manage?'

'I'll be quite happy to wipe it all off and let you do it yourself, if you'd rather,' Shae returned evenly, already reaching for the pot of cleansing-cream.

Marianne shot her a look of pure venom, but shook her head.

'This will have to do. I don't have time to waste sitting around and letting you practise your minimal talents on me.' She stood up and walked from the room without so much as a backward glance, and Shae looked down at her hands, surprised to find they were trembling, though they'd been rock steady just minutes before. Well, she'd faced up to and conquered one major challenge in dealing with Marianne—but that trauma would seem nothing when she was forced to face Dane. The very prospect made her spirit quail.

'Hi, Shannon. Ready for me?'

The unexpected male voice at the door made her heart race, but she was able to summon up a smile when she found herself looking into Gavin's hazel eyes.

'Sure. Come on in.'

His arrival seemed to set the conveyor belt in motion, and she lost all track of time as she dealt with one actor after another, flinching every time the door opened, yet aware of a peculiar emptiness when Dane failed to show up. The rest of the cast seemed blissfully unaware of his absence, and not one questioned her about her own disappearance. Once again she felt a rush of warmth for Josh; clearly he'd gone to some lengths to cover up for her, and for that she'd be eternally grateful. Right now she was incapable of concocting any kind of explanation, and she certainly couldn't have faced telling them all the truth.

She was just bending over to pat powder on to a young actress's face when she heard the door open behind her and a strange tingle of apprehension prickled the back of her neck. She didn't need to turn round to know he was standing there, and it took all the will-power she possessed to finish the task she was working on, knowing he was just a few feet away.

'There you go,' she said at last. 'Twenty-first-century woman.'

The young woman laughed a little shakily.

'Thanks, Shae. You've done a terrific job. I just hope I'll do half as well on stage tonight.'

Shannon patted her shoulder comfortingly as she rose from the chair.

'Course you will. Now go and relax in your dressing-room for a little while—try a few of those deep-breathing exercises you've been telling me about. They should help steady your nerves.'

As she left the room, Shae slowly turned, her heart hammering in her chest like a jungle drum as she came face to face with Dane. His expression was unreadable, his features more cruelly hawklike than ever.

'Why, Shannon?' He spoke quietly, yet she trembled as though he'd struck her. 'Why this time? What made you run?'

She could barely believe he could ask her such a question. How had he expected her to react to his betrayal—with laughter, perhaps, or nonchalance? But this was neither the time nor the place for a showdown—the score would have to be settled later.

'Never mind that now.' She tried to sound brisk, but the tremor in her voice was unmistakable. 'You've got a play to do, and I haven't even started your make-up yet.'

'Damn the play and damn the make-up,' he returned harshly. 'I've spent the whole day searching for you.' He took a step towards her, and it was all she could do not to back away from the menacing look on his face. 'Now I want answers.'

'Not now, Dane. Look, I came back because of the play. Because I couldn't let everyone down. You can't either.'

His eyes narrowed dangerously as he stared down at her.

'"Because of the play?"' he echoed mockingly. 'Are you really so sure that's why you came back, Shannon Lea?'

Before she could answer he grabbed her by the shoulders and pulled her against him, his fingers biting cruelly into her skin. She tried to struggle, but he caught her flailing wrists and pulled them roughly behind her back, holding them easily in one hand. The other snaked into her hair and she tried to twist away from him, her eyes blazing in fury, but he was too strong, and his mouth claimed hers in a kiss that was brutal in its intensity. She was scorched by his touch, branded by his lips, and the fight suddenly drained away from her, leaving her weak and trembling in his arms.

'All right, Shae,' he said with quiet authority. 'You've answered my question. We can talk later. Now you'd better start turning me into a space-station commander.'

Applying his make-up was the hardest thing she'd ever done, her hands shaking as she smoothed a base coat over his skin. She kept trying to tell herself that his was just another face in a long line of faces, but the nearness of him was agonising, and she was forced to face up to a bitter realisation. No matter what he'd done to her, her feelings for him hadn't changed. She was still in love with the man, and the knowledge threatened to crumble the defences she'd been steadfastly attempting to rebuild all day.

He sat in silence as she worked, and for that, at least, she was grateful, knowing it would be well-nigh impossible to carry on any kind of sane conversation right now. At last she stood back, summoning up a weak, unconvincing smile.

'Finished.'

He shook his head.

'Oh, no, Miss Lea, not finished. Not by a long

chalk.' Then he stood up and strode from the room, and she all but collapsed into the chair he'd just vacated, feeling as though she'd been battered by a storm at sea. She was still there, staring emptily into space, some considerable time later when Josh appeared at her shoulder.

'Well done, Shae,' he said softly. 'I know that can't have been easy for you.'

She gazed up at him through dazed, unfocused eyes.

'Why are you being so nice to me?' she said wonderingly. 'You should be furious that I ran out on you at such an important time.'

He smiled. 'You must have done it for a good reason. But I knew in the end you wouldn't let us down—and I was right, wasn't I?'

'But you barely know me,' she returned curiously. 'How could you be so sure?'

He gave a little shrug. 'Call it instinct, I suppose. I just knew I could trust you. There was never any real doubt in my mind.' He laid gentle hands on her shoulders, his voice warm and understanding. 'Now come on—my masterpiece is in action on stage and we're missing it.'

Standing beside Josh in the wings, she was barely aware of the play being acted out just a few feet away, too caught up in the playwright's words to be aware of anything else. He'd trusted her; even when everything seemed to point against her, and although he'd known her only a few short days, he'd believed in her. That was more than she'd done for Dane, she realised, feeling the first faint stirrings of doubt.

She gazed at the golden-haired figure standing so tall and so proud in the centre of the stage. The kind of betrayal she'd been believing him guilty of was mean, petty-minded, and he was none of those things. But there was no way Marianne could have found out about her past other than through Dane. Questions whirled in her brain as the play progressed, unfolding its tale to an appreciative audience, yet she was no nearer to an answer as the curtain dropped for the final time after the cast had been made to take several bows.

'They loved it!' Gavin's eyes shone rapturously as he ran off stage and gripped Josh enthusiastically by the arms. 'Your play's a wow, Mr Thayer.'

'Let's just wait and see what the critics have to say,' Josh returned drily, but he was grinning broadly, clearly delighted.

'And here comes the star of the show.' Gavin raised his hand in a mock salute. 'Come on, Commander, we've got a first-night party to attend.'

'That can wait,' Dane said grimly, his eyes hard as he spotted Shae half hidden behind Josh's bulk. 'You and I have some serious talking to do first, Miss Lea.' His hand shot out as Marianne attempted to push past, catching her by the wrist. 'And something tells me you're involved in this, too.'

'Me?' The actress turned innocent green eyes up to him. 'But what have I got to do with anything?'

'That's exactly what I intend to find out. Now come on, both of you—move!' He gave Marianne a none-too-gentle shove, grasped Shae's hand firmly in his own, and walked resolutely along the corridor towards the make-up room, ignoring the interested looks of the other actors, and Marianne's attempts to wriggle away.

'OK.' Inside the room he closed the door firmly in

Gavin's disappointed face, and turned to Shannon. 'The truth, Shae. Why did you run away?'

'Because I believed you'd told Marianne about my past,' she said quietly.

'You believed I'd done what?' Incredulous fury shot sparks in his blue eyes. 'In heaven's name, why?'

'Because she told me you had.'

'I did no such thing,' Marianne retorted fiercely. 'I don't know what she's talking about, Dane.'

'Never mind that now.' He waved a dismissive hand in her direction as if she were an irritating fly. 'Do you still believe that, Shannon?'

She met his eyes.

'I don't know,' she said, with painful honesty. 'I don't know what to believe any more. But she knew all about me, and I couldn't imagine any way she could have found out other than through you.'

He remained silent for what seemed to be an eternity, and she turned away with a strangled sob.

'Even now, you don't say a single word in your own defence,' she groaned brokenly. 'Isn't that proof of your guilt?'

'Not guilt, Shae.' He spoke so quietly she was barely able to hear him. 'Hope.'

'Hope?' She stared at him incredulously.

'Yes.' The warmth in his voice reached out to enfold her like an embrace. 'Hope that even after all the anger and the pain you've been through in your life, you'll still be able to search your heart and realise I could never betray you. Hope that for the first time in your life you'll discover trust within yourself for another human being.' He slowly reached out to take her hand in his. 'Hope that you'll finally understand what I've been trying to let you know over the past few days without frightening you away by putting it into words. I love you, Shannon Lea. I'd never hurt you.'

She closed her eyes, buffeted by the storm of her own emotions.

'Well, Shae?'

'I don't know,' she whispered. 'I'm so confused!'

'There's nothing to be confused about,' he returned calmly. 'Either you believe me or you don't. If you don't, then there's really nothing more to say. But if you do, even though the evidence seems stacked against me, it can only be because you love me too, for that's the only thing that could overcome a mistrust as deeply rooted as yours.'

Her eyes filled with tears, but she made no attempt to blink them away, too caught up in an internal struggle which she knew could determine her life forever after. All of her deepest, oldest instincts told her it was crazy to put her faith in any man. Yet—there was an enduring lone voice among the internal babble which held out strong and true for Dane, and somehow its message was the only one that made any sense.

The rest of the room seemed to disappear in a blur as she looked into his face, seeing him as if she'd never really seen him before. She had no idea how long she stayed there, simply gazing into the beautiful sea-blue eyes which had become more important than life itself to her, but everything she saw there somehow made all of her doubts, all of her fears just slide away, leaving her lighter of heart than she could ever remember being. At last she reached up to gently touch his face.

'You're right, Dane,' she said tenderly, allowing

her unguarded heart to speak for the first time. 'I do trust you, and I do love you, though perhaps I'd never really have found that out without this test. I still don't know how Marianne found out about my father and my past—but I know now that you didn't tell her.'

He pulled her into his arms, pressing her close as a long, shuddering sigh rippled through her body. She could have stayed there forever, but after a moment he set her gently aside and turned towards Marianne.

'Now,' he said calmly. 'Which gutter did you choose to go digging in the dirt?'

She looked up at him through thick dark lashes.

'I don't know what you're talking about. And I don't see why you should take that little crook's daughter's word over mine.' Her eyes calculating, she curved her lips into a beguiling smile as she laid her hand on his arm. 'After all that we've been to each other over the years, Dane, darling. . .'

'We've been exactly nothing to each other,' he said curtly, lifting her hand and dropping it as though it were poisonous to touch. 'I've known just what sort of a woman you are ever since the first time I was unfortunate enough to meet you—though I confess I didn't realise even you could stoop quite as low as you have this time.' He regarded her steadily. 'Now I'm going to ask you again; where did you find out about Shannon?'

She glowered sulkily back at him. 'I really don't see why I should tell you.'

'Beacause if you don't, I'll ask Josh to throw you out of the cast—and somehow I don't think you'd enjoy that, my little prima donna. Just think what the newspapers would make of that!'

'Oh, very well.' She sniffed haughtily, gathering her shreds of dignity about her as best she could. 'It really wasn't so very difficult, though your precious Shannon seems to believe her sordid little secrets are locked away in a safe somewhere.' She fixed Shae with a baleful glare. 'I saw the look on your face in the coffee-bar when Gavin said you'd better beware of skeletons in your cupboard—frankly, it was a dead give-away that you had something to hide.'

She shrugged uncaringly. 'After that it only took a single phone call to a friend on the television station in the north where you used to work. She told me you left the station because someone arrived who could let your secrets out, and you couldn't bear the shame.' Her eyes glittered maliciously. 'Incidentally, that person must have rather a big mouth, because your shameful little secret's public knowledge there now.'

'There is no shameful secret,' Dane cut in harshly. 'What her father did has nothing to do with Shae. One day she'll understand that for herself.'

'She's a nothing and a nobody,' Marianne snarled, her voice laden with resentment. 'She'll drag you down into the gutter with her, Dane—but if that's all you want from life, then damn you.' She turned on her heel and stalked out of the room. The very air seemed sweeter after she'd left.

Dane's lips quirked in a smile of wry amusement.

'Well,' he said, taking Shae in his arms and softly kissing her hair, 'it would seem I am damned, because you are indeed all I want from life.'

'Are you sure, Dane?' She gazed up at him, still half afraid to believe what was happening. 'Marianne was right—I am a nothing and a nobody.'

'Hey!' He gave her a mock-ferocious scowl. 'I'll

have you know you're insulting the woman I love. I'm the only one who's allowed to do that!'

'But you could have any woman in the world. Why me?'

He smiled. 'Lord knows. But when I found you'd run away from me again, it nearly sent me crazy.'

She laid her forehead against his chest, drinking in the warm masculine essence of him.

'I had to come back,' she said quietly. 'I told myself it was because of the play, but deep down there was something driving me back to you.'

'I'm afraid Marianne will take great delight in telling your story, Shae. Not now, when she knows I'm watching her every move, but eventually.'

Shannon allowed the thought to sift through her mind, expecting to feel the usual pain, but there was none. In a strange way, she felt cleansed, as though she'd been able to strip the dark places away from her soul.

She laughed wonderingly. 'As crazy as it may sound, I don't think I really care any more. Not if you're with me. That's all that matters.'

His arms tightened about her.

'I'll always be with you,' he swore. 'Now and all the days of my life.' He slanted a playfully mischievous smile at her. 'Not forgetting the nights, of course.'

Feeling deliciously secure and wanted in his embrace, Shae slid him a teasing look.

'You never did tell me just exactly what you and Marianne had been to each other in the past.'

Dane grinned sheepishly. 'I'm afraid that was a deliberate ploy on my part,' he admitted. 'I thought if I planted a few seeds of jealousy in your mind it might just drive you into my arms that little bit sooner.' His eyes grew serious. 'But the truth is, there was never anything between us—not after I'd discovered she cared more for her mirror than for anything or anyone else.'

He gave a little shrug. 'The snag was, she found it impossible to accept that anyone could possibly find her less than addictive. I hurt her pride and she was never able to come to terms with that. But you, Shannon Lea—you are the only woman I've ever loved, the only one I ever will love. You're in my soul forever.'

She turned her face up for his kiss, her heart singing within her as their lips met in a caress that was both healing and passionate. With this man at her side, she would never walk in shadows again.

Mills & Boon